# Let Sparks Fly

Beverly L. Anderson

Phoenix Voices Publishing

# Contents

# INTRODUCTION

Welcome to this group of short stories! I hope you enjoy them! Here you will find two stand alone stories, a six-part novella, and three stories based in the Chains of Fate series. If you want more information about any of them, check out my website! It's linked at the end of the book.

## Trigger Warnings

Consensual Non Consent
Graphic Sex
BDSM Scenes

# Green Pleasures

Flynn and Evie had been dating for quite a while and went on a picnic, inviting Avery along. He'd hesitated initially because he honestly didn't want to have to watch them having sex again. He'd already walked in on that too many times at the apartment he shared with Flynn. Granted, he didn't mind the view when it happened. They promised it would just be a picnic and nothing would happen. Still, Avery didn't quite believe them. He agreed, though, and knew he would probably regret it. He had no idea what would happen but had a foreboding feeling.

They arrived at a nice glade near a sparkling pond. Flynn and Evie chatted as they brought out the blanket and laid it on the grass.

"Avery, I hope you're hungry! We brought plenty of food!" Evie said, bright blue eyes sparkling as she pulled the picnic basket out of the car and handed it to him.

He grunted as he took it because it was heavy. Wondering how Evie could sling it around so easily since she was so petite, he picked it up anyway. He shook his head and took it to the blanket where Flynn had just flopped down on the corner as he brought it up. He was tying his long brown hair up in a bun.

"Bastard, you could carry the heavy things," Avery groused as he sat the basket down.

"But you did such a good job of it!" Flynn said with a wink of his dark brown eye.

"Uh huh," Avery grumbled as he sat down. He glanced up and saw Evie approaching with drinks.

"Now, now, you two, be nice!" she said, kneeling on the blanket and opening the basket. "We came here for a nice quiet day in the sun, so let's make the best of it!" she handed a plate from the basket to each of them and set one out for herself.

They ate sandwiches and had some teacakes that Evie had made for them. They chatted about school and how their college courses were going. Flynn was going to business school with Evie, and Avery was trying to get into medicine. They shared classes, though, for the core curriculum. All three of them had taken the same psychology and biology class this year. They'd been friends since high school, and Flynn and Evie had been a couple for just as long.

As he expected, Flynn started touching her a little here and there, and looking at her in that way, that Avery knew what was coming. Only this time, he had nowhere to escape to. With a sigh, he got up and went to the pond. He heard Evie giggle now and then and wondered how long before they forgot entirely that he was with them. He had grown accustomed to being the odd one out for a while.

Sticking his hand in the water, he waved it around. The pond was surprisingly clear, he noticed, and he saw fish and floating plants in it. He looked into the water and saw his reflection. He blinked, though, because his reflection changed, becoming a pale copy, it seemed. Reaching up, he put his hands on his face, and the reflection moved the same way, but then the eyes in his reflection bled into a strange color of purple that glowed and one of them winked at him. He sat back and gasped. What was that? Did he just see that?

Looking over, he saw that both Evie and Flynn were quite occupied in kissing each other senseless. His breath was a little heavy as he leaned over and looked back into the pond, seeing his reflection this time unchanged. What was going on? He stood up slowly, looking around and wondering what exactly that was and why it was happening. He heard something in the trees. It sounded like someone walking around in the small glade.

"Hello?" he called, walking around the pond and toward the wood. "Is someone there?" he asked quietly. He heard Evie giggle again and knew they weren't watching him at all.

"Follow me…" a voice said from the wood, giggling in an echoing voice.

Avery frowned, glancing back over to Evie and Flynn again, seeing they had laid down on the blanket. He could already see Flynn had his hand up her skirt, and it wouldn't be long before they were even further occupied. He turned back to the wood again.

"Who are you?" he asked, stepping toward the trees.

"Come on, don't be shy…" the voice said, and again he heard the rustling in the trees like someone was moving in them.

This was crazy, he thought to himself. What if it was a killer or something? He couldn't help being curious, though, and he wanted to see who or what was talking to him. Taking a tentative step into the trees, he saw they grew thicker as they went further back into the wooded area. He pushed the branches away and began picking his way through the roots and leaf-covered paths. Again, he heard the high-pitched giggle coming from all around him.

"Your friends know how to have fun," the voice said again. He couldn't pinpoint the direction it came from at all. "Do you?"

"What do you mean? Who is there?" he asked, brushing a limb out of his face as he stumbled and fell through into a perfectly round clearing. It was only about six feet across, but nothing grew in the circle except a coating of soft moss. "What's this?" he gasped, standing up again.

He turned and tried to go back the way he'd come, but found the branches were covering the path now, and he couldn't move them anymore. His heart sped up in his chest as he frantically looked around the small clearing. He walked all the way around it and couldn't find a way through the branches. It was like they were steel and not wood because none would give in the least. The trunks of the trees were close together, and the limbs crisscrossed to make an impossible barrier.

"Help!" he called out, but he could hear his voice bouncing back to him as though inside an empty room. "Someone?"

He'd quit hearing the breeze, and it was eerily quiet now. In fact, the loudest noise was his own breathing. He had no idea what was happening, but he was getting a little afraid of this because this was anything but normal. And if Flynn and Evie were having sex again, they weren't going to notice he was gone.

"Why are you scared? Your heart beats like a rabbit being chased by a wolf. Are you the rabbit, and I the wolf?" the voice asked again, tapering off with a giggle.

"Who are you? Where are you? What do you want from me?" he asked, turning around in a circle and seeing nothing but the trees and the sunlight streaming through the branches overhead.

Again, the strange giggle and then movement as Avery turned around to see a pearly white form coalescing through the trees. His eyes went wide because it looked like him. Only the skin and hair were light green, and the eyes were purple and glowing with a fierce light. The figure even looked to be wearing a white version of the t-shirt and jeans he was wearing. At his feet, vines and thick, leaf-covered branches writhed like they were alive.

"Avery is your name, human," the being said, smiling at him with a wicked grin.

"H-human? What are you?" he stammered, backing up against the trees, but there was nowhere to go.

"What am I?" he asked, tilting his head to the side. "What do you think I am?"

"I don't know! You tell me!" Avery snapped, frowning at him. It was weird looking at someone that was like a green-colored version of himself.

"Hmm, well, I've been called the Green Man before," he said slowly as he glided forward, the vines and branches following with his movement. "Maybe I'm a forest god. Or perhaps a spirit of the wood. Maybe I'm one of the fae. And humans make me very curious," he said, now close enough to reach out and touch Avery's arm. He tilted his head to the side. "Ah, it seems your friends have engaged in some intense sexual activity. Should I join their fun?"

"What? No! Leave them alone!" Avery told him, frowning deeply.

He turned back to him and grinned. "Oh, I should leave them alone, but what am I to do?" he said, frowning mockingly.

"I don't care what you do, but don't you touch them!" Avery growled out.

"You don't care if I do something fun with you?" he asked, smiled again as the frown melted off his face.

Avery's eyes went wide. "What? No! That's not what I mean!"

"Don't lie to me," he said, and Avery felt the vine wrapping around his ankle and crawling up his leg. "You see, you can't lie to me. I see everything you think I don't. I forged a bond with you the minute you touched me in the pond, and I can see into your mind very clearly."

"What do you mean?" he said, getting a little breathless, feeling another vine coiling around his other leg.

"I see your desire. Every time you look upon the male's body, you wish that instead of your female friend, he was laying you down. I see all right here," he said, pressing a finger to Avery's forehead.

Immediately, the dreams and thoughts he'd put away about Flynn over the years, ever since high school, flooded his mind. The slight jealousy he had toward Evie that she got to have him and his tendency to stare too long when he accidentally walked in on them, watching Flynn's muscular body in the heat of ecstasy, came to mind in flood. He gasped as he blinked, locking eyes with the strange white copy of himself.

"Such an imagination!" the creature breathed, leaning in closer, almost touching his lips with his own. "I can imagine a way to satisfy you," he said, breathing out a breath that smelled of fresh mint.

Avery's heart was pounding in his chest, and he didn't know what to do. This was wrong! This was a copy of his own body, so how could he even be thinking some of the things that were going through his mind. He flinched as the green creature reached out with one hand and placed it against his face. He stared into the strange eyes, and his breath hitched in his chest.

"Your mind is so clear, and look here," He told him, sliding his hand down against his front and pressing against the hardness he found there. He licked his lips, and Avery was interested in finding his tongue was blue. He then leaned forward and came very close to him again. "I just need your permission."

"M-my permission?" Avery stammered.

"Yes, your permission," the green creature said, sliding his hand up and under his t-shirt. "I'm not a fiend."

"What am I giving you permission to do?" Avery asked, worried a little about what he meant to do.

"Give you pleasure beyond your wildest dreams as you fulfill my desires," he said, running his hand up to pinch at Avery's nipple. "I know your wants and can ensure you get all you want."

"What are your desires?" Avery said with a glance around him where more of the vines were beginning to gather.

"I desire you; don't you understand?" he said. "Just say yes, and I'll give you an experience you'll never forget."

Avery didn't know what to do. He didn't even understand what this creature was, but he couldn't deny his arousal at the thought of being pleasured by him. Just having the thoughts of Flynn brought to his mind had made that happen. It wasn't like he could ever express his attraction to his best friend. He and

Evie were probably going to get married, and then where would he be? He sighed out, knowing what he wanted.

"Yes," he whispered. "Please..." he told him.

"Good, good," the green creature murmured as he reached out and pulled Avery's shirt off over his head. Avery just let him do it without a thought. He then felt his fingers on the buttons of his jeans. His breath kicked up again as he watched those black-nailed fingers deftly undo the button and zipper. The vines wrapped around his calves released and slithered up to slide down into his jeans and ease them off his hip. His shoes popped off his feet as the vines worked his pants over his body. He was a little embarrassed because he wasn't wearing underwear today.

"Hmm, look there," he said. "Humans usually wear layers, but you only have one."

Avery blushed then, but vines rose from the ground and entwine his arms now. He struggled against them a little, panicking a bit.

"What are you doing?" he asked when he couldn't move his arms. Another vine wrapped around his waist and pulled him up off the ground above where his clothes had pooled.

"Just a little fun," he said with a grin as he stepped back to watch as the vines entangled his body, binding his arms behind his back and pulling his legs apart. "You look lovely like that," he breathed, moving over and rising from the ground on the vines.

"Please, what are you doing now?" he asked, knowing there was no way he was getting out of this.

"You gave your permission; now allow me to follow through on my promise. I cannot break a promise; it is against the rules." He reached out and pressed lips against his neck, laying biting kisses there.

"Rules, what rules?" Avery asked, pausing to moan at the sensation of someone teasing the sensitive flesh of his neck.

Another vine slipped down and wrapped around his cock, causing him to jerk. He gasped as the thin vine wound around the base tightly, and then another slid under his balls and squeezed them tightly. He was panting a bit now. The creature left his neck and found his mouth. His tongue easily pushed into Avery's mouth and began probing him deeper than any human tongue would have been able to. In fact, it felt as though his tongue was filling his mouth and brushing against the back of his throat.

As he felt his hands slide around and begin playing with his nipples, he nearly choked on the vine-like tongue. He pulled back, his tongue sliding back out and slithering into his mouth like some snake.

"Every part of that which moves is me," he explained as Avery felt one of the thicker vines rubbing between his legs. "I am in every piece of this wood."

Slowly, the vine rubbed against his entrance, making him whimper at the sensation. It was new and he'd never been touched by anyone else there before. He flicked his wrist and the vine penetrated him smoothly, small at first, then widening the deeper into his body it went. He moaned at the pleasant pain that the stretching brought him. Then it thrust back and forth, seemingly lubricated by some source because it wasn't rough at all.

"There, how's that feel?" He asked, fingers still pinching at his nipples. "It feels hot and tight to me inside you. Can you take some more?" he asked.

Avery gasped as he felt it plunge deeper, growing even thicker as it did so. "P-please!" he said finally. "It's too much! I can't take it!"

"Oh, I can read your mind just fine, and you can't hide how good it feels." He then thrust the vine into him a little more before pulling it back and slipping into him again. "Now, I'll do something to make you feel even better," he muttered.

Avery panted a little openly as he looked down to see delicate vines moving around his cock and then beginning to slide down into the tip. He squeaked at the feeling. "What is that?"

"Just a little more fun," the creature told him, holding his hands out and controlling the small vines that began sliding into his cock.

Avery threw his head back and let out a sound he didn't know he could make, feeling his body filled up like this. He needed to come but he couldn't with the vine wrapped around the base as tight as it was. Then he moaned deeply as he felt the one inside his ass begin rubbing something that felt incredibly good. He giggled again.

"Ah, there we go. I found the spot," he said, and Avery felt more pressure on that spot, which felt so good.

Avery couldn't articulate anything near coherent as he was reduced to a mess of sounds. He moaned deeply. This creature moved again and began kissing him, his tongue sliding deep into his mouth and nearly choking off his air. But it felt amazing, and he wanted more and more of it. The thrusting vine inside him pumped back and forth at a pace that he would not have been able to stand had he not been held up by the vines. The ones that had filled his cock were also thrusting down into him. He mumbled around his tongue as he tried to beg to be allowed to come.

It seemed to take a long time, but finally he pulled back his tongue and he looked at him. Avery was panting with his tongue lolling in his mouth.

"Oh, my, have I broken you yet?" the creature asked, running a hand over his head, threading fingers through the blond locks.

"I need...I need... Please!" he managed.

"Oh, do you need to come?" he asked, kissing his throat as he pulled his head back. "Just a second," he said, slipping a hand down and stroking him firmly.

Avery wriggled in the tight bindings he was in and whined deep in his throat. Slowly, he felt the vines that had slipped down into his cock work their way back out of him. The one thrusting into him so deeply gave him no pause. It simply rubbed directly against his prostate until he arched his back and felt like he was coming. It felt different, and it brought no relief when it was done. He was still hard, and nothing had come out.

"A dry orgasm," the creature mumbled. "How nice."

Avery whimpered pitifully because he ached from the need by now. The creature waved his hand a little and the vine constricting the base of his cock let go. He sighed in relief as he felt the most intense climax he'd ever felt come rushing at him. He relaxed completely in the grip of the vines holding him up. The creature's hands slid over his oversensitive body.

"There, there," he said, wrapping his body up in vines and limbs.

Avery had never felt something like this. It was like his mind was simply existing without being required to do anything at all. He felt the gentle caresses of his hands or vines or both. He was secure, warm, and comforted. He had never had an experience like that before, and he had nothing to compare it to. His mind faded out and for a while he knew nothingness.

He gasped and sat up suddenly, sitting alone in the circular clearing. He was in his clothes, but his body left no room for doubt about what happened. But where had the green creature gone? He looked around and saw the clear path back out of the clearing and back to the pond. He slowly got up, wincing as pain lanced through his back. He looked at his arms and saw light red marks where he'd been bound. It was all real. Everything that had happened had been real. He just knew it.

He walked toward the pond, the path clear and easy to follow. He came out and glanced down at the water, only to see his own reflection staring back at him.

"Avery!" he heard. He looked up. "Where were you?" Evie said, waving at him.

"Um, just took a walk," he said softly.

*More than a walk* came a high-pitched voice in his head. *Tell them what you want.*

He couldn't say such a thing, he thought to himself. He couldn't tell them what he wanted more than anything.

*Yes, you can.*

"Avery, are you alright?" Flynn asked.

"C-can we talk?" he asked suddenly as he approached the blanket where they were sitting.

"Sure, what is it? Look, if it's about a little while ago, I'm sorry, things just kinda went that direction, and well, you know," Flynn said, running a hand over his bright red hair.

"I have to tell you something." He sat down beside Flynn on the blanket. "This might ruin our friendship, but I can't keep this up anymore."

Evie kneeled beside him and took his hand. "What do you mean, Avery?"

"I'm sorry, but I've loved Flynn since high school and could never say it, and now I don't know what to do with these feelings. Every time I see you together, it makes my heart break into pieces because I see what I can't have," he rushed through without looking at either of them.

*That's a good boy.*

Neither Evie nor Flynn said anything,, and Avery didn't know what to do. Tears in his eyes spilled over and fell onto his hands, where Evie still held onto him. She hadn't let go.

"Oh, Avery," Evie whispered and squeezed his hand.

To his surprise, Flynn's hand went into his lap and grasped his other hand. He looked up to see him staring directly at him.

"Since high school? And yer just now sayin' something?" he said softly.

"I'm sorry," he whispered. "I know you're going to marry Evie probably, and it isn't fair of me to do this, but I can't keep it to myself any longer. It's tearing me up inside."

"What does me marryin' Evie have to do with this? This is something else entirely." Flynn pulled his hand over toward him and looked at him.

"What do you mean?" Avery asked, looking up at him.

"Avery, why do you think you're always with us?" Evie said softly. "We consider you a part of our family already."

"B-but I want to do more than be family," Avery whispered.

"I know, Avery. We both know and have for a long time," Evie told him.

Avery looked over at her sharply. "What?"

"You haven't been hiding it very well," she explained, interlacing her fingers with his. Flynn did the same to the other side, twining his fingers in Avery's.

"Wh-what do you mean? You knew?" he stammered, looking between the two of them.

"Yer kinda dumb sometimes," Flynn said with a sigh before reaching over and brushing his hair over his ear. "But that's alright. I—we love you anyway."

Avery turned to him, and his eyes really overflowed with tears. "Y-you mean that?"

"We were just waiting for the right time to bring it up, but it never seemed to come," Evie said.

"B-but I don't want to do things with you like I want to do with Flynn..." he started.

"I know, and that's okay. I don't mind sharing him with you because I love you so much, too," Evie said, kissing his hand.

He turned back to Flynn. "And you're okay with this?" he asked.

Flynn leaned forward and pressed his lips against him. Avery's eyes widened at the feeling, but his mouth opened, and Flynn slipped his tongue in quickly. He let go of Evie and wrapped both arms around Flynn's neck, holding on tightly as he kissed him like he'd always wanted to. He pulled back and grinned at him.

"What do you think?" he whispered. "Now, you've started something, but are you willing to finish it, is my question?"

Avery frowned in confusion for a second, and then he felt Evie's hand slide over his crotch, where he had become very interested in kissing Flynn. He jerked a little and looked down. "I think he can finish things, don't you?"

"Here? Now?" Avery asked, eyes wide again.

"Here. Now," Flynn confirmed, grabbing Avery's hand and pressing it against his own tightness in his pants.

It didn't take long before Flynn had Avery's clothes stripped off him, with a bit of help from Evie. She seemed to enjoy participating in everything as he helped where she could. Flynn had already been stroking him and working him up to the point he was already about to come unglued. He then laid him on his back on the blanket, sliding between his legs and looking down on him.

"Might be a little harsh without any lube, you sure?" Flynn said.

Avery nodded, Evie brushing his hair out of his eyes as she sat beside his head. "It's fine, just do it!" he exclaimed.

Flynn smirked and spat on his hand before he spread it on his cock. He quickly pressed against Avery and slid himself in at once. Avery arched off the blanket, grasping at the ground until Evie grabbed both his hands and held them down. He breathed heavily, and despite the pain, it felt so good, too.

*Knew you'd like it.*

He wrapped his legs around Flynn as Evie held down his arms. Flynn thrust into him hard and fast, roughly stroking him now and then as he did so. He was big enough that he felt so full of him and while it wasn't like the green creature's vine-dick, it was still amazing, nonetheless. He found himself coming and Flynn just kept on until Avery found himself hard again. This time, Evie helped by stroking him as Flynn slammed into him harshly.

*Aren't ya glad I fucked you already and loosened ya up some?*

Avery was very glad, actually. He didn't know if he could have stood Flynn doing it without lube otherwise. Finally, Avery nearly yelped as he came over the edge again, this time pulling Flynn over with him. Then they fell into a panting, sweaty mess of limbs.

A couple of hours passed, and the sun went down as they all packed up to go home. Flynn had told Avery he could stay in their bed tonight with them, and he couldn't believe it. What had happened was beyond anything he could have imagined. , as in his dreams, he had been

*I'm with ya from now on. I've bonded to you already. But only you will know my presence. And know it, you will.*

Avery didn't know what exactly he meant by that, but he would soon figure it out as in his dreams he was visited by a very familiar greenish, vine-wielding figure.

# Stray Cat Chronicles
## Part One

## A Stray Cat

The first day of swim class, Leslie Kirby knew he was going to hate having his partner. He got stuck with a taller guy named Aaron, and he was weird. He had a tattooed sleeve on his left arm that started at his shoulder and ended at his wrist. The entire thing was a pattern of panthers, skulls, bones, and grim reapers. Then he had a huge back piece that had one black panther as the centerpiece surrounded by a jungle or a forest background. All the tattoos were full color, and Leslie had to wonder where a college student got all the money for such things. He even had piercings. His ears were each gauged, and he had an industrial bar piercing in the upper area of his ear on the right, and two other piercings on the left. He also had a ring in his left eyebrow. This, paired with his size, made him quite imposing. He was, overall, a rough looking individual. In fact, he even rode a motorcycle to school every day.

The biggest problem that Leslie had was that he thought the guy was hot. He had a trim, strong body, and while broader than most swimmers, he had tremendous upper body strength and powerful thighs. He had the clearest blue eyes he'd ever seen, and curly blond hair that was shaggy about his head and laid in kinky curls when it was wet. Leslie hadn't thought much about any of his swim class companions until he was face to face with his new partner. Now, he had to deal with being attracted to the guy he was supposed to swim with on a daily basis over the semester. He briefly wondered if he could still get out of swim class...

"I can't believe you got us thrown out of class! Again!" Leslie growled as they stormed back into the locker room, running his hands through his short, damp brown hair.

"If ya weren't such a dumbass and were able to stop arguing in front of the coach, we wouldn't have this problem!" Aaron snapped back at him.

"Me? You're the problem!" Leslie hissed at him.

"I told you that you were doing the stroke the wrong way and it was going to get you injured, but ya can't take criticism!" Aaron pointed out.

"I can take criticism just fine from anyone but you!" Leslie exclaimed, crossing his arms and sitting down on the bench in a huff.

"And why is that? What's so wrong with criticism from me?" Aaron grumbled, standing over him with his arms crossed as well.

Leslie looked up at him and felt the blush start forming before it could even be seen because he was standing over him. He turned away and muttered something under his breath that Aaron couldn't catch.

"What was that? I don't understand mumble."

"I said, it's because I'm attracted to you, okay?" Leslie finally managed, still not looking at him.

"Yer what?" he asked, surprised. "Yer gay?"

"I'm not gay or straight. See, you think it's gross and now you know, so we really can't be partners anymore," Leslie said, frowning now, but still looking away from him.

Aaron didn't say anything for a minute and Leslie was afraid he was going to get punched or something. He was frankly surprised he hadn't, or Aaron hadn't left in anger. Of course, they were both still in their swimsuits. Which made this even harder because of the way the flimsy material clung to every curve on Aaron's body, and he was trying very hard not to stare at him.

To his surprise, he felt a hand against his cheek. He stiffened, thinking he was going to get hit, but instead, Aaron's thumb swept over his lips. Shocked at the gentle touch, Leslie looked up at him, dark brown eyes wavering between tears and not.

"Is that all that's wrong with ya?" Aaron asked, pressing his thumb at Leslie's lips, then slipping it into his mouth when his lips parted.

Leslie looked a little surprised, eyes widening as his tongue sought out the intruding digit in his mouth. As Aaron pushed his thumb deeper, he kept his eyes focused on Leslie's, just staring at him until a smirk spread across his face.

"Ya suck that nicely. What else can you suck nicely for me?"

Leslie could immediately and without a doubt see that he'd acquired Aaron's interest. He himself was sitting with his legs squeezed together trying to disguise his own problem just from Aaron touching him. It was incredibly intimate just having his thumb probing into his mouth like this.

"Come on," Aaron said, pulling his thumb out of Leslie's mouth with a slight Dad. He reached into the locker and grabbed his shower bag and pulled Leslie to his feet. Next, he unlocked one of the shower stalls and swung Leslie into the small space outside the shower. "Now, let's see what you can do with that mouth of yours," Aaron growled, reaching out with both hands to pull Leslie's face toward him.

Leslie gasped out as Aaron dove onto his mouth. His mouth open, Aaron's tongue easily plundered his slack jaw. He had never kissed anyone before, and he most certainly had never kissed someone with tongue before. He found the initial contact to be a bit slimy feeling, but that sensation quickly faded as his tongue responded and twisted with Aaron's. His body felt loose as he leaned against the wall of the stall as he pressed both hands flat against it. Then Aaron's hands began to slide down the outside of his arms until they came to his hands, where they interlaced fingers with him. He pressed back as Aaron pressed down, using his height difference to his advantage in the situation.

When the need for breath won over them both they pulled apart reluctantly, Aaron placing his forehead against Leslie's and breathing softly still holding to his hands. Leslie's own breath was heaving in his chest, and he didn't know what to do right then. He knew that he had never been this aroused in all of his life and he wanted to keep kissing Aaron desperately. He licked his lips, locking eyes, brown on blue, and couldn't keep the near gasping of his breath quiet.

"What if... What if someone comes in here?" Leslie finally stammered.

"Class just started. We got at least an hour. The question for you is how much of a slut are you for me?" Aaron asked, moving his hands to slide one down to rub at Leslie's crotch. "You're damn hard and soaking through your swimmers. Just how bad have you been wanting this?"

Leslie let out a whimper, feeling Aaron's hand against him was like fire. Then he slipped his hand down inside the front of the suit, hand gripping him tightly and causing him to moan out loud. Aaron only grinned, stroking him with his hand a few times. He slid his other hand around and slipped it in the back of the swimsuit, squeezing at his ass with surprising gentleness. Leslie was about to come undone already and he'd barely touched him.

Then, Aaron let go of him in the front and slid his hand around to squeeze at his ass again with both hands this time. He ground forward, rubbing his own trapped hardness against Leslie's. He rubbed against him a few times before releasing his ass to move his hands around to free himself from his suit. Leslie looked down at him and felt his heartbeat rise a little more.

"On yer knees," Aaron growled, pushing down on Leslie's shoulders.

He went, slipping to the floor in front of him and felt his mouth watering at the prospect of actually sucking on Aaron. He panted as Aaron thrust his hips forward and pressed against his lips. Without thinking more of it, he opened his mouth a little and Aaron shoved himself forward, nearly choking him in the process. He came off and coughed for a second into his hand and wondered if he could actually do this.

"Relax, yer too tense," Aaron said. "If you don't relax, things won't go so smoothly."

Leslie nodded, leaning up and taking just the head into his mouth this time, rolling his tongue around it. He found the place just under the head to have some effect on him as he slipped the tip of his tongue against it.

"There ya go," Aaron whispered, hands buried in Leslie's hair. "Just take in as much as you can, Leslie-babe. Nice and slow this time."

Leslie managed to take more of him into his mouth, but when he hit the back of his throat, he gagged and pulled his head back some. He concentrated on not scraping his teeth against him, feeling him press at the back of his throat. He knew some people could swallow all the way down, but he didn't think he could try that sort of thing yet. He whined a little as he felt Aaron pull up on his hair. He looked up at him and wondered what he wanted him to do.

"C'mere," Aaron said, and Leslie stood back up again. Had he done it wrong? He didn't think he was that awful.

There was a shelf about waist high along one side of the stall. Aaron pushed him to lean over it. Then his hands were on his hips, slipping the swimsuit down off his hips toward the floor. Leslie blushed a bit, being completely naked now in front of him.

"Yer so cute, getting embarrassed at me seeing ya without yer clothes on, when you were just on yer knees a second ago sucking my cock," Aaron commented, grinding against Leslie's ass with his arousal. "I'm gonna go on unless you tell me not to."

Leslie wanted to tell him to stop in some ways, but he didn't want him to stop any more. Not stopping won in his brain due to the throbbing in his own cock. He jerked as he felt Aaron's hand slide down and begin to probe at his entrance gently. He gasped a little at the sensation of having anyone touch there. But it felt kind of good at the same time as it felt a little strange. Then he saw him reach for the bag he'd brought with his shower stuff in it. He fished around in the bag and pulled out a yellowish colored bottle with a spout on the top of it. He pumped some into his hand and went back to pressing against him. He could smell the distinct scent of cocoa butter; it was lotion. It was cold as he slipped a finger into him coated with the lotion. He whined at the back of his throat because that felt strangely good.

"Look at that, ya slut. Already moaning after I put a finger in yer ass. What are you gonna do when I shove my cock in you?" Aaron asked him as he plunged his finger back and forth in him.

"I can't... You can't... That won't go!" he stammered, squirming as he felt him slip another finger into him.

Again, he let out a barely contained moan as he felt it stretch and burn a little. "It'll go. Your tight little ass is already sucking in two of my fingers with a little lotion on them. My cock ain't much bigger than that."

Leslie had no response to that other than to bury his head in his arms and stifle another loud sound that threatened to escape his lips. He couldn't contain the things that his body was doing, and he had never felt like this before. He nearly squealed when Aaron's fingers started rubbing against something that felt really different.

"Hmm, there it is," Aaron muttered over him, and Leslie had no idea what he was talking about. He knew it felt good, though. "I thought I could find it."

"What... What is that? It feels weird!" Leslie exclaimed, trying to keep his voice at a whisper and not succeeding. If anyone walked into the locker room right then, they'd be found out immediately. As if two sets of feet in the shower stall wouldn't tip anyone off.

"Just yer prostate, Leslie-babe," Aaron murmured in his ear. "Feels good, don't it?"

"Hah!" was the only response Leslie could give.

For a minute or two, Aaron continued to torture his prostate, ruthlessly stroking it without pause until Leslie felt like he needed to come, but it felt weirder, and it wasn't centered in the front like usual. He whimpered again, finding the sensations too much almost.

"Please!" he finally begged.

"Please what?" Aaron asked, teasingly.

"I don't know!" was all Leslie could manage as his voice descended into another low, throaty moan.

"Hmm, well, I know I can't wait any longer," Aaron finally said and pulled his fingers out of him slowly.

Leslie was panting against his arms, feeling the sensations that had been building start to fade a little. It was mildly frustrating because he'd felt close to orgasm before he stopped. Now, he was left with a throbbing arousal that was not letting him forget the position he was currently in. He turned his head to the side, seeing that Aaron pumped more of the lotion into his hand. That meant he was going to try it? A sudden fear flashed through him. What if it hurts? What if he didn't like it? He sure had liked what he was doing a second ago, though, so he couldn't imagine not liking it...

"Here, move your hips a little," Aaron told him, adjusting him until he felt the pressure against him where he leaned into him. "Just relax; it won't hurt unless you tense up."

Hoping he was speaking from some sort of experience, Leslie tried to relax his body but was finding it decidedly difficult. Then he was pushing, and he felt him entering his body and it felt strange and invasive at the same time as erotic and thrilling. He bit the back of his arm lightly as he whined out loud. He thought he was never going to stop pushing forward. His body felt full and like it was on fire at the same time.

"See, it fits just fine, what do you think?" Aaron asked, leaning over him now, holding himself still inside him.

"Feels good," he managed. "Feels weird. I don't know!"

Aaron chuckled and began to pull back and push forward again. Leslie gasped at the sensation and scrabbled on the side where he was leaning. It didn't really hurt, but he could feel him sliding in and out of him and that was enough to set him on edge. Then, he moved and started pressing against that same spot that his fingers had found before. He whimpered out loud again and practically melted as Aaron's hands slid around and began stroking him lightly. It wasn't very tight, just teasing him a little.

"You sure this is your first time? Because you're quite the slut already," Aaron muttered in his ear. "Or is that just because it's me?"

"Just you," he panted, feeling like he was just going to keep edging him until he couldn't stand it anymore.

"Ah, well, I'm glad to hear that. I'd hate to have to hurt anyone that touched you before me," he replied, slamming his hips forward and making Leslie moan again as he slipped against his prostate. It seemed he was in the right position to hit it.

"You like this, don't you?" Aaron asked, thrusting into him steadily. "This getting fucked in the locker room like some whore?"

"Please...I need to... to..." he started, unable to finish the sentence as he panted heavily.

"Aw, does Leslie-babe need to come?" Aaron teased, slowing down his thrusts significantly and releasing Leslie in the front.

"Ah, no, no, please, no!" Leslie gasped as he stopped touching him. "Please! Don't stop!"

"Aw, how can I resist such a slutty demand," Aaron growled and sped up again, leaning around and stroking Leslie steadily along with his thrusting.

Leslie's body was thrumming with energy, and he needed to let go. But was it long enough? Had he held on long enough for Aaron to be satisfied? He wasn't sure. Then Aaron grabbed his face and turned it toward him, latching onto Leslie's mouth from the side and probing deeply with his tongue. Leslie stiffened, whimpering into Aaron's mouth as he came suddenly in his hand.

Aaron let his mouth go and smirked. "Now, why'd you come right then?" he asked.

Leslie dropped his head into his arms again and moaned as Aaron sped up once again, coming to completion seconds later. He pulled out and flipped Leslie around, pinning him back against the ledge and grabbing him in another deep kiss. He just relaxed into Aaron's arms and let him explore his mouth again, his own tongue lazily meeting him now and again. Aaron finally pulled back and looked at him with heavy breaths.

"Ya need to shower, and so do I," he mumbled pulling Leslie into the shower stall.

They shared Aaron's shower supplies and washed each other slowly as the water ran down on them. If they'd had more time, it might have led to some more fun, but they were pushing the end of class as it was. They both managed to get out and start getting dressed just as the rest of the class came into the locker room. If anyone was curious why they were just now getting dressed, no one commented, though more than one person had an idea what had gone on.

They left together that day, and every day from then on, they came to class and left together. There were no more fights between them in front of the coach and everyone who had eyes could tell they'd gotten together. No one mentioned it, of course, but everyone knew that the stray cat had found a home.

# Stray Cat Chronicles Part Two

## Bringing a Stray Home for Christmas

"Dad," Leslie said into his phone. "Um, so I'm bringing home someone I've been seeing for Christmas this year..."

"Oh, you are? Who is she, my son?" his father, Blake, asked immediately.

"Um, well, his name is Aaron..." he started.

There was the expected silence on the other end of the line. His father cleared his throat. "Him? You're bringing home a boy, are you?"

"Yeah, we've been dating a while now, and it's as good of a time to meet everyone as any. He's got nowhere to spend the holidays and I told him that you'd welcome him. Right, Dad?" Leslie asked.

"Of course, of course," Blake said. "He's more than welcome, but if you stay the night he'll have to sleep on the floor in your old room or on the couch."

"I think the floor is more comfortable than the couch, Dad," Leslie quipped.

"That's true, my son. Your mom, Beatrice, and Hailey are looking forward to seeing you then. So, we'll see you Christmas evening, then?" Blake asked, and Leslie could tell he was trying to keep his voice even.

"Yeah, I'll see you Christmas. We should be there by around four. We're taking his motorcycle from the city as long as the weather holds out nice," Leslie explained.

"Motorcycle?" Blake said, sounding a little unsure. "Well, uh, just be safe, okay?"

"Always, Dad. See you Christmas!" he said and clicked off the phone.

He stood there, standing beside the bed staring at the phone in his hand for a long while.

"That didn't seem to go as bad as you thought," came the rough, deep voice of Leslie's boyfriend, Aaron.

He turned around, smiling at him. "Yeah, it did go pretty well. He was surprised, but I gotta wonder how he'll react to seeing you, he's a doctor after all."

Aaron was taller and a little broader than Leslie, but Leslie only stood five feet eight inches. He had a sleeve on his left arm from shoulder to wrist that featured panthers, skulls, bones, and grim reapers. He had piercings in his ears, including small gauges, his eyebrow on the left side, and his tongue. He tended to favor t-shirts and ripped jeans with riding boots and leather jackets.

"Does being a doctor mean that he has a thing against tattoos and piercings?" Aaron asked with an arched brow.

Leslie sighed and looked at him. Meanwhile, Leslie was Aaron's opposite. He wore button down shirts or polos with slacks during the winter. The exception was he did have a pair of jeans now that he went riding with Aaron now and then, as well as a thick leather jacket. They often rode, even when it was pretty cold, as long as there was no snow on the ground. This year had been especially good for riding because it had stayed relatively warm and snow-free.

"No, it just means he expects things, and he might be a little put off because of your appearance. But I'm sure once he gets to know you, that'll change," Leslie said, sitting down on the bed.

"You think he's going to think ill of me just off m'looks, huh?" Aaron said with a smirk.

"Well, you are scary to people that don't know you," Leslie said as he crawled over into Aaron's arms. "I know you, though."

"Hmm. We staying the night there?" Aaron asked, running a hand through Leslie's hair.

"Yeah, dinner won't be until late, so we'll have to stay there the night. I hope that's alright?" he said with a glance above him at Aaron's face.

"Of course, Leslie-babe, of course."

* * *

Blake was a little nervous Christmas evening. Everyone slept in, of course. There was no reason to get up early without little kids around to open presents first thing in the morning. The girls were seventeen and nineteen this year, with Beatrice being the older of the two. She'd already started university like her brother, and Hailey would be going next fall. Their brother. He hadn't told the girls that Leslie was bringing home a guy. He was honestly surprised, but he wasn't going to say anything. Whatever his son wanted, he would support him. He wandered into the living room and saw the girls sitting on the sofa watching a Christmas special. Their mother, Georgina, was snoozing in the chair beside them. Of course, she already knew about this.

"Uh, girls?" Blake said as he came into the room.

"Yeah, Dad?" Beatrice said, turning and looking at him.

"I should probably tell you that Leslie is bringing someone with him to Christmas dinner today, someone he's been dating it seems," he started a bit nervously.

Beatrice and Hailey exchanged a look, then both grinned. "He's got a girlfriend?" Hailey said excitedly, smiling broadly.

Blake knew that she was imagining making a connection with another girl that was older, and he had to warn her that wouldn't happen. "Um, well, not exactly..."

"Not exactly?" Beatrice asked. "If he's dating someone, isn't it his girlfriend?"

Blake sighed. "Um, well because his name is Aaron."

Both girls stared at him for a minute. "A dude?" Beatrice asked, wide-eyed.

"Leslie is dating a guy?" Hailey gasped, putting both hands over her mouth in shock.

"Yes, and I want you to treat him just like you would treat any girl he ever brought home. You never know, he might be a great guy," Blake said with a shrug.

Beatrice frowned. "I don't know about this."

"Well, just be nice to him, and try to understand that he had nowhere else to go for Christmas. So, we just have to be good hosts for him," Blake explained.

Beatrice narrowed her eyes at him. "Alright, but if he's not good for Leslie, I'm not going to like him. How long has he even been dating this guy? He didn't just start dating him, did he?"

"I really don't know how long; he never said anything about it to me. We'll just have to take it one step at a time." He looked over and saw the time was getting close to four. "They should be here soon. They were taking Aaron's motorcycle."

"Motorcycle? In December?" Beatrice asked, crossing her arms over her chest.

Georgina woke up then and looked over and smiled at Blake. She nodded, indicating he should keep on going with what he was doing. Georgina had been ill the last month, a slow growing cancerous lung tumor that she was going through chemo and radiation for. Her prospects were good, but Blake let her rest rather than expect her to do anything around the house.

"They said if the weather was nice, which it has been," Blake said.

"They better have helmets," Beatrice muttered and turned back around to watch the tv show.

"I'm sure they're safe," Blake said. "I'll go check the food and make sure the ham is doing well. Once it's done, I'll put in the pies. Then it should be dinner time by the time everything is done."

"I'll take care of the pies, Dad," Hailey said as she turned back to the television. Then she turned around and looked at Blake again. "Does this mean Leslie is gay?"

Blake smiled at her. "I don't know, that's something for him to say."

About half an hour later there was a knock at the door. Beatrice looked at the door and Hailey jumped up to go answer it.

"It's Leslie!" she said excitedly as she ran over and pulled the door open. She gasped a little and stepped out of the way to let them in. "Hi, Leslie, and um, Aaron, right?" she said, and Beatrice thought she sounded a little off.

Beatrice got up and went to the door and immediately froze. This was the guy her brother was dating? He was taller than Leslie by a bit, and as he took off his leather jacket, she could see his arm was completely tattooed. She could see piercings as well.

"Yeah," he said and Leslie waved at Beatrice where she stood in the doorway.

"Um, I'm Hailey," Hailey said to him and gestured toward Beatrice. "And that's Beatrice."

"Nice to meetcha," he said with a grin.

Leslie was also wearing a leather jacket but his wasn't as bulky as the one that Aaron had just taken off. He slipped out of his and took Aaron's from him to put them both on the hook by the door. He turned and smiled at Beatrice.

"Hey, Beatrice, Hailey," Leslie told them. "Um, good to see you. How's mom?"

"Is that my wonderful, amazing son?" he heard and Leslie rolled his eyes as Blake came around to the doorway.

"Yes, Dad, who else would it be?" he asked.

Blake glanced at Aaron once then looked at Leslie. "Ah, I take it this is Aaron?"

"Yeah, Aaron, this is my dad, Blake Kirby," Leslie told him. "Mom should be in the living room."

Aaron put out his hand and Blake took it. "Good to meet you, Mr. Kirby. I appreciate you letting me come," he said.

Blake took his hand and shook it. "Um, yeah, nice to meet you, too. Please, come in," he said as he stepped back into the house. "How was the ride from the city?"

"Oh, good, Dad. The weather turned out perfect for it. It's nice and warm in the leather jacket Aaron got me for Christmas," he said, smiling at him.

"Oh, well, that's good," Blake said. "Please come into the living room, have a seat. Aaron, you can meet Georgina, their mom. We'll talk a little bit. You'll have to tell us about yourself, Aaron," he commented as they came into the living room.

Aaron and Leslie sat down next to each other on the smaller of the two sofas, and Beatrice, Hailey, and Blake sat on the other one. Georgina sat up and smiled. Leslie went over and hugged her tightly and had a short conversation about her health before he returned to his seat.

Once everyone was seated, Blake looked over at Leslie and Aaron. "So, tell me, where did you two meet?" he asked.

Leslie looked over at Aaron then at Blake. "Well, we were in the same swim class last year. We didn't like each other at first, as a matter of fact, we both got sent out of class for fighting with each other a couple times over the semester. Then, one day after we'd gotten sent out to the locker rooms before class was over, it just kinda happened and we've been seeing each other since then," he smiled and took Aaron's hand in his.

"Oh, that's interesting," Blake said with a bit of a forced smile. "Um, so what are you going to school for?"

"I'm actually going to business school, so I can run my own mechanic shop. I already have an associate degree in auto tech, and I have my certification, so it was just a couple more years to get a business bachelor's degree," Aaron answered.

"Oh, well that's nice. Do you already work?" he asked.

"Yeah, I have a full-time job at a place in the city. They're cool, though, they work me around my school schedule." He squeezed Leslie's hand. "Good thing is, I get weekends off, so we can go riding and do stuff."

Blake nodded. "Ah, I see. That's...nice. Do you do that often?"

"Oh yeah, Aaron takes me all over the place. We just get on the bike and drive for a long time then see where we end up," Leslie said with a smile. "It's a lot of fun."

"Dad, I'll go check on the pies," Hailey said suddenly, standing up and going into the kitchen.

"Pies? That sounds good," Leslie said with a smirk. "I haven't had anything sweet in a while. Been trying to stay in swimming shape."

"Yer too thin as it is," Aaron grumbled, turning and looking at him. "Ya worry way too much about your weight."

Leslie sighed, turning and smiling over at Blake. "Alright, I'll eat a lot today, just for you, okay?" he said, patting Aaron on the leg thoughtfully.

Blake cleared his throat and looked over toward the kitchen. "Are things alright in there, Hailey?" he called.

"Yeah, I think the pies are ready; I'm taking them out," she answered.

"I should go help her get the rest of the food started. The ham is in the roaster and should be ready by about five. Why don't you stay here and chat with Beatrice and Georgina?" Blake stood up and headed into the kitchen.

Beatrice was glaring at Aaron without trying to hide it. Leslie turned toward her. "So, how is school going this year?"

"Good," she answered. She still glared openly at Aaron.

"Have you been playing soccer lately?" Leslie continued, trying to get Beatrice onto any subject possible except Aaron. He knew she'd probably be upset with him.

"Yeah," she answered, then grit her teeth for a second. "Been practicing with the college team. Doing really well this year. We're off for the winter, of course."

"Yeah, figured that, but I bet you still go out and practice even if it's cold," Leslie said with a smirk at her.

Beatrice nodded. "Yeah, that's true enough. Excuse me, I need to use the bathroom," she said and got up.

Georgina cleared her throat. "Don't mind her, she's rather protective of her brother," she said with a wan smile. "I'm terribly sorry, but I think I'm going to go to bed. I'm not feeling well at all," she said, standing shakily.

Leslie got up and hugged her. "Take care, mom. I'll come see you in the morning before we leave," he said.

Georgina nodded and headed up the stairs with painful slowness. Leslie watched her go and then sat back down.

After they were left alone Leslie let out a sigh. "Going better than I thought," he mumbled.

Aaron took his hand again. "They seem nice. A bit spooked by me, though."

"Well, you spook most people," Leslie muttered.

"Yeah, well, you know, what can I do," he responded, leaning in to kiss Leslie's cheek.

After a while, when Beatrice didn't come back, Leslie got up and wandered into the kitchen where Hailey and Blake were busy preparing the rest of the meal. "Can we help with anything, Dad?" he asked.

"Oh, no, son. Just relax and we'll get everything taken care of. Your, um, boyfriend seems to be really nice. Already got a good job, too," Blake commented as he pulled the ham out of the roaster oven.

"Yeah, I think he likes you all. I wonder where Beatrice got off to?" he said as he turned and left the kitchen to go back to the living room.

A few minutes later, Beatrice came down the stairs and into the kitchen. She had a scowl across her brows. "What's wrong, Beatrice?" Blake asked as he carved the ham into slices.

"What's wrong?" she hissed. "That...that guy is what's wrong! Do you see him?"

"Now, Beatrice, he's been perfectly polite and hasn't said anything untoward. You should give him a chance and not base your opinion on his looks alone," Blake said, as though telling himself as much as he was telling Beatrice.

"But Dad!" she started.

Blake held up his hand. "No. Treat him like anyone else that's been a guest in our house, and no different. He may look a little rough, but your brother seems to care about him."

Beatrice snorted and turned around to go back to the living room. She tried not to look angry for Leslie's sake, but she couldn't like this guy because he obviously wasn't good enough for her brother. She sniffed and sat back down on the sofa again, trying to put a smile on her face.

"Sorry, had a friend text me," she said, trying to look nonplussed.

"Oh, that's fine. I was just telling Aaron about our mom," Leslie said, and Beatrice almost said something she'd have regretted. Instead, she smiled tightly.

"Oh?" she mumbled.

"Yeah," Leslie said, pointing out the pictures on the wall of them when they were younger. "He doesn't have any family at all left himself."

"All I got left is an adopted sister named Anna. I was raised in foster care, bounced from house to house," Aaron explained.

Beatrice did feel a twinge bad for him. Being a foster kid was tough. She was trying really hard to do what her father said, but it was difficult.

"Dinner's ready, kids!" Blake called from the kitchen.

"Okay, Dad, we're coming," Leslie said, standing and taking Aaron's hand to lead him.

Beatrice walked behind them and promised herself she was going to be nice during the rest of dinner. They all sat down, and Hailey had already put out plates for everyone. Blake set out the rest of the food with the large ham as the centerpiece of the table.

"This looks wonderful, Dad," Leslie said as he settled into his seat. Aaron sat beside him.

"You outdid yourselves this time," Beatrice said as she sat on the opposite side of the table. Hailey would sit beside her, and Blake would sit at the head of the table between Leslie and Beatrice.

Once everything was out on the table, and everyone was settled into their seats, Blake looked around. "How about we each give one reason we have to be happy this holiday season?"

"That sounds like a good idea," Leslie said with a grin. "Want me to start?"

"Sure, son, go ahead," Blake told him.

Leslie cleared his throat. "I'm happy to have such a wonderful and accepting family that cares about my decisions as much as you do."

Blake smiled and looked at Beatrice. "What about you?"

"Um, well, I'm happy that Leslie could come home for Christmas with us," she said, looking over at him but avoiding looking at Aaron.

"Me next!" Hailey exclaimed. "I'm happy because the school year is almost over and I'm going to be graduating soon!"

Blake smiled and nodded, turning toward Aaron. "What about you, Aaron?" he asked.

Aaron thought a minute, then looked at Leslie. "I'm happy I found Leslie when I did. If it weren't for him, I wouldn't be where I am now."

"And I'm happy to have all of you here for dinner tonight!" Blake exclaimed and clapped his hands. "Let's eat!"

Dinner itself was idle chatter around everyone talking about how good everything had turned out. Beatrice actually engaged in some small talk with Aaron and Hailey finally seemed to be coming out of her shell around him a little bit. Leslie tried to stop eating and Aaron chided him, telling him that he needed to eat more than that. All in all, the dinner itself was comfortable and peaceful. After everyone had finished, Blake and Hailey cleared the table and brought out the pumpkin and cherry pies with the whipped topping for it. Leslie tried to refuse, but Aaron glared at him. He ended up splitting a piece of each with Aaron.

After dinner and dessert was done, and everything was cleared off the table, Blake asked if they all wanted to play some spades. Everyone was interested in joining a game except Aaron, who didn't know how to play. So, he ended up sitting with Leslie and watching how the game was played and played his first game instead of Blake with the next hand. Everything went well, and by the time they realized it was too late to go home, the sun had already set.

"Well, you'll have to stay the night, then," Blake said. "Here, I'll get some covers and the sleeping bag for the floor of Leslie's old room. I'd suggest the couch, but honestly, the floor is more comfortable."

"We packed a change of clothes in the saddlebags," Leslie said. "I'll go get them."

While he was gone, Blake was left alone with Aaron. He didn't know what to say to him at all, so he didn't say anything. He hadn't expected his son to be the first one to bring home a boyfriend, and he was still getting a little over the shock of the whole situation. Leslie came back into the house with a drawstring bag full of clothes that had been in the saddle bags.

"Here we go. We'll at least have something for in the morning," Leslie said with a smile at Blake.

"I put everything on the floor in your room, son. I'll let you two get some sleep," Blake said, leaving them to go up to Leslie's room.

As soon as they were in and the door closed, Aaron grabbed Leslie and pushed him up against the back of the door, leaning in and kissing him deeply. Leslie, surprised, went with it and responded to him quickly. Aaron pulled back and looked at Leslie, a little breathless.

"Been dying to do that all night," he breathed.

"Well, I'm glad you kept yourself in check until we were in private," Leslie said, breathing a little heavily himself.

"Yeah, it was close. You have no idea how bad I wanted to pin you over that table," he growled into Leslie's ear as he nipped lightly at the lobe.

"Ah, what are you doing?" Leslie muttered, relaxing into the hold Aaron had on him a little bit.

"What do you think?"

"We can't do that! I mean, not here!" Leslie gasped.

"Why not?" Aaron asked, sliding a hand down between his legs and finding him interested.

"What if they hear?" he whispered hoarsely.

"Yer an adult, ya can do whatever you want, what does it matter what they hear?" he asked.

"It's my family, Aaron, we can't just..." Leslie trailed off in a whine as Aaron's fingers got his slacks open and he slipped his hand down in his boxers.

Aaron smirked and stroked him firmly a couple times. "And what about this?"

"That's your fault!" Leslie hissed. "All the kissing and grop-ing!"

"Then let me take care of it," Aaron said, leaning in and kissing his neck, using his slight height advantage to great effect.

Before he could say anything else, he was kissing Aaron again, this time hungrily and needy. The next head spinning motion took him to flop on his back in his bed. It was only a twin, so there wasn't a lot of room. However, they were used to the small confines in Aaron's room already.

"Shh," Leslie hissed as he heard the bedsprings groan a little.

"You're the noisy one, so you shh," Aaron grumbled as he managed to wrestle Leslie's shirt off him while he squirmed a bit on the bed.

Leslie felt Aaron's hands glide over his chest, pausing to flick at his rapidly hardening nipples. Then he slid the slacks and boxers down off his hips.

"Already debauched?" Aaron muttered as he undid his jeans and kicked them off followed by his own boxer shorts.

"Shut up!" Leslie said, almost too loudly.

"Better be quiet, or your sisters are going to hear you," Aaron reminded him, reaching down and stroking them both together slowly.

Leslie clamped both hands on his mouth to stifle a moan that nearly escaped. "And you want me to be quiet. You can't keep that whore mouth closed, and I know it."

Leslie whimpered as Aaron slipped one hand down and pressed two fingers roughly into him without warning.

"Ah!" Leslie exclaimed.

Aaron chuckled lightly, twisting his fingers inside him until he was pressing and stroking Leslie's prostate. After a few seconds, Leslie started humming and obviously trying to keep his voice down. Aaron didn't give him any chance to stop as he pulled his fingers out and got up between his legs, sliding into him swiftly.

"Oh my god," Leslie gasped this time, managing to stop himself from yelling.

"Listen to you, you're already moaning like a slut. You can't even keep your voice down in your father's house, can you?" Aaron whispered hoarsely into Leslie's ear.

"I can!" Leslie growled back, biting down on his lip until he could taste blood. That was going to be sore in the morning.

He could barely contain the heavy moans that wanted to escape his lips. He began humming louder to try and cover it, but that was getting too loud now, too. Suddenly, Aaron clamped his hand over Leslie's mouth.

"You're going to let them all know how much of a slut you are if you don't keep your mouth shut," Aaron growled, slowly thrusting into him and steadily working him into a deeper set of sounds.

"I...I can't help it!" he gasped as soon as Aaron moved his hand, grabbing his head and yanking him down into a kiss, thinking he could occupy his mouth and stay quiet. It worked, at least for a couple minutes.

It was becoming obvious that Aaron was going to make this last because he wasn't hurried at all. He wanted to draw Leslie to the edge of his very ability to control himself, and then take him over that edge. He wasn't touching him at all, so he was intent on dragging it out as long as he himself could hold out. And Aaron had the stamina to last when he wanted to.

"Listen to that, you can hear the sounds coming from you no matter what you do," Aaron said, kissing him again, then sitting back up and pushing Leslie's knees toward his shoulders, giving him an even better angle and new set of sounds as Leslie bit down on his knuckle this time. "Those sounds belong to me, not anyone else, so keep your mouth shut, understand?"

Leslie whined again, this time a little louder as he wanted to cry out more, but he couldn't. He never realized how hard it would be to try and not be vocal during sex. It was like every motion sent a shiver through his body that wanted to come out in a pleased moan. And Aaron's constant talk wasn't helping matters; it just made him want to make noise worse.

"Look at you, trying so hard, and you're dripping worse than I've seen you in a while. Are you this turned on by doing it in secret like this?" he said as he began to slowly stroke Leslie as he slowed down again. "Do you really want your family to know what a slut you are for me?"

"N-no," he murmured, trying to keep his voice down. "I don't..."

"Then shut the fuck up and be quiet," Aaron growled, pulling back and slamming forward hard enough to get a surprised squeal out of him. "Listen to that!" he hissed back at him.

Leslie whimpered, biting into his lip again. He couldn't say anything at all because if he did, he was going to cry out louder than he wanted to. Instead, he held on as Aaron's hand glided over him, stroking him in time with his slow and steady thrusts. Leslie was going out of his mind with the need to come and the need to yell out Aaron's name at least. He never realized how much he talked and made noises until he couldn't make any sounds at all.

"Are you gonna come like my good slut?" Aaron asked, slowing even more.

Leslie nodded his head furiously, still biting his lip to avoid crying out. "What was that? I can't hear you?" Aaron teased, almost stopping in his motions.

"Yes!" he gasped, arching his back a bit and rolling his hips to try and get Aaron to move faster again.

"Yes, what?" Aaron asked, starting to thrust into him a little faster as he spoke.

"Yes, I wanna come," he whined.

"Like a what?" he asked, stroking Leslie a few times before he leaned forward and nuzzled into his neck and laid a set of biting kisses on his chest.

Leslie felt his face flush even more. "I don't know!"

"Yeah, you do. You know what to say," Aaron said, leaning up and pushing his legs a bit wider.

And it was true. Leslie knew what he wanted, but he wasn't sure he could get it out without nearly screaming it. He was being driven mad at this rate with the way he was edging him.

"I...I wanna come...I'm your... slut..." he panted out, not sure if he could hold it any longer, and held back a loud moan, but just barely.

"Good, good," Aaron said, starting to speed up as he spoke. "So, come for me, like the good slut you are."

Leslie couldn't hold on a minute longer; he felt the orgasm slam into him and he shoved his knuckle back into his mouth as he hummed against it. He felt Aaron go over seconds later, tightening his grip on his legs as he did so. He pulled back and slipped down beside him in the bed. Leslie was panting, one arm over his head.

"You managed to be fucked without moaning like a whore the entire time," Aaron said with a sly smirk.

"Shut up. Whose fault is it?" he complained, putting an arm over his rapidly reddening face.

"I don't think I like not hearing you," Aaron said, plucking Leslie's arm off his face and kissing him again. It rapidly deepened to a consuming thing that left them both breathless.

"I'm glad you suggested the clothes, your shirt is soiled," Leslie pointed out.

Aaron nodded and pulled the shirt over his head and used it to wipe Leslie's stomach off. "Yeah, so it is."

"We should sleep," Leslie said. "Stay up here, we can snuggle together on the bed if we both lay on our sides.

"Alright, let's get under the covers and get some sleep."

They adjusted themselves under the covers and both quickly fell into a deep sleep despite the tight confines of the bed. A short time later, the door opened, and Blake looked in to see the two of them curled around each other, peacefully sleeping. He quelled the part of him that reminded him that his son was sleeping with another man as if it were wrong. There was nothing wrong with them. They were perfectly fine just the way they were.

# Stray Cat Chronicles
# Part Three

# A Stray at Midnight

"**A**re you sure about this? You said you wanted to wait," Aaron said as he sat on the desk chair backwards watching Leslie.

"Things went good when we met my family together, so I think it's time that we stopped keeping things a secret," Leslie said as he looked through the closet. "I'd wear those sparkly jeans but they're a little loose..." he muttered as he pulled out a pair of jeans that were dusted with sparkles on the sides. "I've never worn them."

"How come they're a little loose? You just bought them a couple months ago," Aaron said with a frown.

"Just been working out a lot at the pool is all," he responded, setting the jeans out. "But they're not that loose. I can pull them down without unbuttoning them, but if I wear a belt, they should be fine."

He went back into the closet and looked for a shirt. Aaron glared at him, starting to worry again. Just last week at the Christmas dinner with Leslie's family, he'd had to encourage him to eat enough. Now, he was losing weight? Something was going on.

"What are you going to wear?" Leslie asked as he looked through his T-shirts.

"Just the usual. I don't see any reason to change up just for a little New Year's party. Aren't your friends gonna be surprised when I show up with ya?" he asked, watching as Leslie pulled out a pair of shirts from his closet.

"Well, next semester, we're getting an apartment together. That's only a few weeks away," he said, gesturing to the boxes already packed with his stuff.

"Seems kinda sudden though, just to show up to a party with a boyfriend ya ain't told no one about before tonight," Aaron mused.

"They'll be surprised, that's for sure!" he said, holding up a shirt with a stylized skull on the front of it. "What about this one?"

"Looks fine, Leslie-babe," he said, smiling gently at him. He was so worried over what he was going to wear to this party. He was as bad as a chick sometimes.

Leslie stripped off down to his undershorts to change. Aaron couldn't resist, though. The temptation was too high, and he had no idea how he was going to make it through tonight if he had to keep his hands to himself. He got up and stepped behind him as he was about to pull the T-shirt over his head. Quickly, he slid both hands around his chest and pinched at both of his nipples. Leslie squeaked, as usual when he surprised him.

"What are you doing? We don't have time for that! The party's in an hour!" he complained.

"Ah, I can wear what I'm in, and yer clothes are here. We can have a little fun before we go. Might make the night easier on me waiting until we're alone again and I can really ring in the New Year the way I want," he growled into his ear, sliding his hands down the flat plane of his stomach to rest on his hips.

"We haven't got time!"

"Alright, alright, but I plan to ring in the New Year my way after this party with yer friends," Aaron grumbled stepping back and letting him get into his clothes.

"Yeah, you can do whatever you want after the party," Leslie said, turning and kissing him quickly.

Aaron arched a brow. "Promise?"

"Promise."

A sly smirk spread across Aaron's lips as he looked into Leslie's brown eyes. "I'll hold ya to that."

Leslie shook his head and went into the bathroom to try and do something with his hair. It just seemed to stick out at every angle no matter what he did with it. Aaron thought it was cute that he constantly tried to get his hair to behave even when he knew nothing was going to work. He went and sat back down at the computer chair and waited. Again, he thought how much like a chick Leslie could be sometimes.

"Alright, I'm ready!" he said finally, coming out and buckling the belt on.

"I'll follow your lead, whatever you want to tell them when we get there, I'll play the part. Just in case you change your mind about coming out in front of 'em," he said with a soft grin.

He knew that Leslie wouldn't do it. He worried far too much about his friends and what they thought of him. He was okay with that. His friends didn't have to know that he was being fucked into every surface Aaron could push him up against. Then again, they'd never been to a party with alcohol before. They'd never been to a party, period.

"I'll tell them!" he asserted, but Aaron already knew better. Nothing would change tonight at all.

They took the car this time as it had gotten way too cold this week for the motorcycle. It was a nice, small four-door car that Aaron had bought with his first job. Leslie gave him directions to a really nice house in an affluent area. He looked at it.

"Wow, I stick out here," he said, letting out a soft whistle.

"No, you don't, come on, there's so many people for you to meet!" Leslie said excitedly as he hopped out of the car.

Aaron couldn't help but smile a little bit. Leslie's excitement was a bit infectious. They walked up the long path from where they'd parked up by the house. They could already hear music from within. Leslie grinned at Aaron as he pushed the button for the doorbell. A few seconds later, a guy with black hair answered it.

"Yo! Leslie, you came!" he said with a grin, then his eyes settled on Aaron. "And you brought a guest!"

"Yeah, Aiden, this is Aaron, my..." Leslie trailed off and hesitated a second. "My, uh, friend!"

Aaron nearly snorted because he knew when it came down to it, he wouldn't admit that he was his boyfriend. "Yo," he said instead.

"Oh, nice ta meet ya," Aiden said and reached out a hand and shook Aaron's.

"Same," Aaron said.

"Come in! You can meet some more of the others. Leslie's never mentioned you before..." Aiden said and they came into the foyer.

The whole place was decorated with sparkling decorations. The foyer led into an open living room where there was a large lighted ball hanging, almost like a disco ball, reflecting light all over the room. There were people dancing in an open place in the center of the room to the music. There was a stand set up nearby where someone was playing on a DJ station. Aaron had never seen such a huge house.

"Come on, Micah's in the kitchen. Drinks are out if you want one," Aiden said over the loud din of the music.

They came into what was perhaps the biggest kitchen that Aaron had ever seen. There was a short girl with dirty blonde hair and deep blue eyes dressed in a sparkly black minidress. She turned and looked as soon as they came in.

"Leslie!" she exclaimed and came over to hug him. "Long time, no see! You've been so busy with school, you haven't been hanging out!"

"Um, yeah, school stuff," Leslie muttered. He cleared his throat. "Ah, this is Aaron. He's, uh, my friend."

"Hi!" she said brightly. "Want a drink? I've got about every alcohol known to man thanks to my brother's stocked bar."

"Sure," he said with a smirk. "I'll take a jack and coke."

"Good man," Aiden said, clapping Aaron on the back. "So how you know Leslie?"

"We're in the same swim class together," Leslie interjected. "We're...uh...gonna be roommates soon, too."

"Ah, that's cool. Guess you can keep Leslie out of trouble!" Aiden said with a smirk.

"So, Aaron, was it, what do you do in school?" Micah asked as she handed him the drink.

"I'm studying business right now. I wanna open my own mechanic's shop," he answered, sipping the drink and cutting his eyes over at Leslie who looked nervous. "You gonna drink something?" Aaron asked him.

"Oh, yeah, um, you have stuff for fuzzy navels?" he asked, blushing a tad, much to Aaron's satisfaction.

"Oh, yeah, forgot you liked fruity drinks," she said, and Aaron coughed and turned his head to keep from busting out laughing right then.

Leslie stared at him wide-eyed for a second then laughed nervously. "Um, yeah!" he said.

"Oh, Emily is here..." she said and winked at him. "I'm sure she'll be happy to see you. Maybe you can get a kiss at midnight after all!"

Leslie laughed nervously again, taking the plastic cup from her and sipping it to cover his reddened cheeks. "Ah, I know she's always had a crush on me, but hasn't she found someone to her liking yet? You know I don't date friends."

Again, Aaron nearly choked on his drink, getting Leslie's attention again. "Um, anyone else here?" he asked, meaning people he knew of course.

Micah glanced at Aaron curiously and back to Leslie. "Ah, yeah, Jackson, Archie, their girlfriends, Rosie, her boyfriend, Joe, Dominic, and the rest I don't think you're familiar with."

"Alright, you got a drink, now go have fun!" Aiden said, shoving Leslie and Aaron toward the living room where everyone was located.

Aaron found it cute how often Leslie looked at him. He kept his distance, got hit on by a few girls, and watched as this one girl with huge breasts practically smothered Leslie in a hug. He arched a brow and wanted to go grab her off of him. Leslie pushed her off gently and spoke to her for a little while. Leslie led her over to Aaron.

"Aaron, this is a high school friend of mine, Emily."

"Nice to meet you," he said, tipping his plastic cup at her.

"Hi," she said shyly and blushed. "Leslie has never mentioned you before."

"Yeah, new friends, right, Leslie?" Aaron said, smirking at him.

Leslie immediately reddened and bit down on his lip. Aaron wanted nothing more but to take him and kiss him in front of the entire gathered crowd to show everyone just who he was with. He looked up as a brown-haired guy with silver glasses and a tall, though not as tall as Aaron, guy came over.

"Leslie!" the black-haired guy said.

"Dominic!" Leslie answered. "Joe!" he said, looking at the taller one. "Micah said you two were here."

"Yeah, quite a party she throws," Dominic said, eyes falling on Aaron. "And who is this?"

"Oh, um, my friend Aaron."

"Yeah, I'm his friend. How're you two?" Aaron asked, cutting his eyes over at Leslie.

"Good," answered Dominic. Joe simply nodded at him.

"You've known Leslie since high school, too?" Aaron asked, smirking at Leslie the entire time.

"Yeah, we all used to hang out together, then we stuck together when we got to college. Though, Leslie hasn't been around much lately, and I was wondering why," Dominic said, looking over at Leslie.

"Just busy with stuff. School stuff." Leslie said, hiding his face behind his cup.

Dominic looked unsure if he believed him or not. He drank out of his own cup and looked over. "Oh, there's Rosie talking to Archie and Jackson," he commented, nodding toward the nearby people.

Leslie looked over. "I haven't seen Rosie in a long time."

The black-haired girl turned, saw them, and waved at Leslie before she and the two guys came over. "Hey, you came. We were wondering if you were going to make it," she said.

"Yeah, I brought my friend Aaron with me," he said, gesturing toward him. "Aaron, this is Rosie, Jackson, and Archie," he said, indicating first the blond guy and second a dark haired, emo looking guy.

"Cool. I don't think I'll remember everyone I meet here," Aaron said with a grin. "But I'll try."

"Did you already see Emily?" Rosie asked, grinning at Leslie.

"Yes, and you know, I've told you, that's not going to happen no matter how much she wants it to," Leslie pointed out as he went to drink again and found it empty. Aaron reached over and took the empty cup from him and tossed it in the trash along with his own.

For the next couple hours, the scene was repeated several times. Leslie introduced him as his friend and everyone was giving him the side eye. He wondered if more than one of his friends suspected something. Finally, as Leslie was talking with someone else, the first guy he met, Aidan, approached, handing him another drink.

"Man," he said, arching a brow at him. "Leslie shows up to the first party he's come to in nearly a year, brings a new 'friend' with him that he's never mentioned and is moving in with, and stays hooked at the hip with you all night. What's really going on?"

Aaron took a sip from the drink, another jack and coke. "Hey, I'm just here for the free drinks," he said and smirked at Aiden. Aiden didn't look like he believed him at all, though.

"Do you really know Leslie from school?" he asked, looking more than a little suspicious of him all of a sudden.

"Like he said, we met in swim class. Didn't get along at first at all. But things got better as the semester went along," he said, glancing over at Leslie who was being pawed at by a drunk girl. He nearly gave in to his jealousy that time, but he gritted his teeth and drank again to cover it.

Aiden eyed him a little while longer then left him alone. Leslie came back over to him a few minutes later. Aaron pulled him in close and whispered in his ear.

"Told ya. Ya can't admit it in front of yer friends, no big deal," he said. "But they don't know how I'm going to welcome the new year when we get back to my place."

Leslie flushed red again and nodded, not noticing that he was being watched by several of his friends.

"It's a big deal; I'm sorry I'm such a coward," he whispered hoarsely in return.

"I told ya, whatever ya wanted," he answered, leaning back and finding he was being glared at by the short girl named Micah.

"I'll make it up to you," he said with a soft grin. "I promise."

"Kiss me at midnight," Aaron said, arching a brow at him. "Just let them all know at one time and break the girls' hearts that keep pawing at you. You don't know how hard it is not to walk up to you and grab your ass and tell them that it belongs to me."

"Kiss you at midnight? In front of everyone?" Leslie said, blinking in surprise.

"Yeah, I don't care either way, but yer kinda lying to everyone that you consider a good friend, and I dunno if that's a good thing or not. Ya already told your family, and once you tell these people, we ain't gotta be so careful in public anymore. Wouldn't you like me to show the world who fucks you?" Aaron said, looking away as he spoke.

Leslie licked his lips and sighed. "You're right. It isn't fair to you. I'll think about it."

He walked away again, and Aaron saw as soon as he was out of earshot, Micah grabbed him and pulled him aside. He smirked, imagining what that conversation was about. He couldn't hear it, but by the look he was getting from her, he could imagine that Leslie's secret wasn't as secret as he thought. That girl seemed pretty observant from what he could tell.

As midnight approached, some of the people there got drunk, and Leslie had been drinking enough to be quite tipsy. Aaron stopped drinking early on since he was going to be driving them home, but Leslie didn't need to worry about that. As he got drunker, he started being affectionate with everyone. And that was beginning to get on his nerves. He was hanging off the emo guy, and Aaron was resisting a great urge to go punch the guy. He wasn't reacting to him, and he had a girl on his arm. So, they all just put Leslie's behavior off to the drinks.

"You should slow down, Leslie..." Aaron muttered to him at nearly 11:30. He plucked a half-finished fruit drink of some sort out of his hand and took it to the kitchen to dump it. Leslie followed him in there.

"What'd ya do that for?" he asked, wobbling a bit.

"You've had enough," Aaron told him. "Drink any more and I won't let you stay at my place tonight."

Leslie gave him a shocked expression. "Really?"

"Really. You've got enough alcohol in your system as it is. You need some time to let it burn off before we leave."

Aaron didn't notice that they were being listened to by Aiden who was standing just outside the kitchen door. He looked around, and not seeing anyone stepped forward and pulled Leslie into him quickly. He slid a hand down over his ass and squeezed gently.

"I can't fuck you if you're drunk."

"Why not?" he asked with a pout.

"Because it ain't right to do that when you can't say yes or no rightly, and you won't remember it anyway," he growled out near his ear.

Leslie's breath hitched and he nodded. "Okay, okay. I won't drink anymore..." he muttered. He paused, stepping back from him and then grinned. "I have a surprise for you, though."

"Oh, you do?" Aaron asked, letting a wry smile cross his face.

"Yup. At Midnight." He nodded once as though confirming that he was sure of this and turned around to go back into the living room.

Aaron shook his head and followed him out where he started talking to someone again. They offered to get him another drink and he declined, saying that he'd had enough. Aaron leaned against the wall with a cup of coke and watched the rest of the room. He thought Leslie's friends were nice, but if they knew the truth, would they still be so nice? He couldn't tell, but so far, he was seeing no one in a same sex relationship. That didn't mean there wasn't someone who was in the closet, of course.

He glanced at his watch and saw it was about five until midnight. Around the room, all the couples were pairing up, and despite what he said, he felt a little pang of hurt. He had expected the night to go this way, so he didn't know why he was letting it bother him. He'd had a good time, found some new people that he could hang out with, but he was still Leslie's friend. He sighed and was surprised when Leslie grabbed him and pulled him into the middle of the gathering crowd.

"Alright everyone, let's get ready!" Micah shouted from her position sitting on Aiden's shoulders so she could be seen over everyone's heads.

There was chatter around him and the couples started intertwining hands and leaning on each other, holding their cups and smiling as the New Year crept closer. He looked over to see Aiden put Micah down and she was standing on the other side of Leslie now. Leslie grabbed his hand and squeezed it behind them.

"Leslie..." he started.

"Shhh," Leslie hushed him.

"Ten! Nine! Eight! Seven! Six!" Everyone started chanting. He felt Leslie's hand trembling in his and wondered if he'd finally got up the guts to show everyone the truth or if he was still going to hide it. "Five! Four! Three! Two!"

Leslie turned toward him and gave him a big grin. Aaron arched a brow.

"One! Happy New Year!!!" Everyone screamed and around them, the couples began going in for kisses and Leslie grabbed him by the face and pulled him down into a sudden, very deep, kiss.

When they parted, everyone was staring at them, and Leslie's face had turned beet red, and he was covering his eyes with his hand. He still clung to Aaron's hand tightly. Aaron glanced over and saw a bemused grin on Micah's face, and he realized that she must have talked to him about it when they disappeared together earlier. Aiden had a knowing smirk on his face beside her, and everyone else just was shocked into silence.

Slowly, people began to stop looking at them and started milling about again, some sending awkward glances at Leslie and Aaron. No one looked upset or displeased, just very surprised.

"You did it," he heard and looked down to see Micah come up to them.

Leslie, still hiding behind his hand nodded feverishly. "I did. I couldn't watch. Is everyone gone?" he asked quietly.

"No one is staring at you, Leslie," Micah said with a glance at Aaron and back at him.

Leslie moved his hand off his face and smiled at her. "Thanks," he said softly.

"You did it, not me," Micah said and headed back into the crowd.

Aaron pulled him around, twining his hands around and settling them on the swell of his ass. "So that means I don't have to resist touching you no more," he said with a throaty growl.

Leslie shook his head. "I can't believe I did that. In front of everyone!"

"I guess that's one way to come out," Aaron said and kissed him chastely on the lips again.

They managed to get in the door before Aaron started stripping Leslie's shirt off over his head. That was it, though, as they tangled tongues in their embrace. They'd barely gotten from the car to the apartment without tripping over each other's feet. Aaron dropped his leather by the door and pulled his own t-shirt off over his head and threw it somewhere. Leslie's fingers were already working on Aaron's jeans button.

"Whoa, let's get in the bedroom," Aaron muttered, grabbing Leslie's hands. "You clear headed?"

"Yes!" Leslie said with a pout on his lips as he followed him into the bedroom. "I told you, I'm fine now! I think the embarrassment burned all the alcohol outta my system..."

"Hah, well, you sure surprised them, especially that girl that was crushing on ya. She kept giving me the strangest looks afterward, especially when I kept hold of ya," Aaron said as he grabbed the buckle on Leslie's belt.

"I can do it!" Leslie complained but didn't stop him as he slipped the belt off him.

Aaron seemed to have other plans as he took the belt and looked at it before an evil-looking smirk spread across his face. Leslie blinked and then shook his head.

"What are you thinking?" he asked.

"You said anything."

Leslie was beginning to regret that promise. "I did, but you're not thinking..."

Before he could finish the sentence, Aaron had sat down on the bed and pulled Leslie over his lap. His heart was beating fast as he stuttered nonsense to try and get Aaron's attention anywhere but on what he was intending to do.

"You can't!" he managed as he felt Aaron slide his jeans off his hips along with the boxers underneath.

"I can, you've been a naughty little boy and deserve a punishment, don't you?" Aaron was smiling as his hand smoothed over the pale flesh of Leslie's ass.

Leslie didn't know what to do. He was kind of scared by the prospect, but at the same time, the thought kind of excited him too. Was there something wrong with him? The thought of being hit with a belt got him worked up? He knew Aaron wouldn't do it if he really didn't want him to, and he was asking him now. He just had to decide if he wanted to try it or not. He swallowed nervously and decided to play along.

"What do you mean? I didn't do anything naughty!"

He felt Aaron slide his finger down and slip it inside, plunging into him without warning. "Oh yeah? You think so? What about all those girls and boys you were hanging on while you were drunk?"

"I didn't..." he started but then remembered vividly clinging to people while he was unsteady. "Oh, I did, but I didn't mean to!"

"Um hmm," Aaron hummed, sliding another finger inside him, making him moan out loud. "Look at you, moaning like a slut just because I'm fingering your greedy ass."

Leslie didn't know what to say, so he just let out a low hum. Then he pulled his fingers out and rubbed the flesh again.

"I'm gonna make this red, you understand me?" he said in a deceptively gentle tone. "Nice, and strawberry red."

Leslie felt his body reacting, and he knew that Aaron could feel it digging into his leg. He could feel Aaron through his jeans where he laid across him. He took a breath and felt Aaron move then he felt the soft slide of the leather against his skin. He was really going to do it...

He wasn't sure how he was going to react, but when the first hit landed across his ass, he jerked, grabbing onto the bed with both hands. The sting faded out into a spreading warmth that felt strangely good, but he could feel tears in his eyes already.

"You okay?" Aaron asked, taking a minute and sliding his hand against the overheated flesh.

"Uh huh," he managed, gasping a little for breath.

He moved his hand, and he felt the belt again, jerking as the pain once more faded into something else. This time, Aaron didn't stop. He just struck him again. And again. Leslie was about to tell him to seriously stop when he felt his hand again, smoothing against the stinging skin. He pulled him up until he was straddling his lap and facing him. Aaron reached up and thumbed away the tears that had collected in his eyes and smiled gently at him.

"What a good boy," he whispered and leaned forward to kiss him again.

Leslie found himself clinging to him and returning the kiss with a great deal of passion behind it. They sat like that for a while, just holding each other and breathing in each other's breath. Then Aaron moved and stood up, standing Leslie up beside him. Leslie looked at him curiously.

"Get on yer knees up there," he said in a husky whisper.

Leslie nodded, figuring that he was going to take him like that. Instead, when he got on his knees, dropping his head onto his arms, he felt Aaron's hands gliding across his too hot skin again. He jerked in surprise as he felt something warm and wet slide against the flesh. He realized it was Aaron's tongue. He was licking the reddened places with incredible care and gentleness. Leslie panted into his arms, feeling a bit exposed as always in this position.

Then, to his shock, he felt Aaron's tongue slide down the crease until he reached his entrance and began to press against him there.

"Oh, my god!" Leslie gasped out, having never imagined Aaron doing this. He'd heard about it, of course. He'd looked up stuff online, so he knew it was something some people did. He just didn't expect Aaron to do it.

"Hmm, you like that, Leslie-babe?" Aaron breathed out against his skin.

"Ng," he managed but it was only the beginning of a whining sound as Aaron started pressing his tongue into him again.

Leslie could feel himself dripping, and he wasn't sure how long he could continue to last with Aaron rimming him. It was hard to hold off normally, but this was nearly impossible. Just when he was about to tell him he couldn't stand it anymore, he stopped, and Leslie nearly collapsed onto the bed.

"Hmm, I'd say that was well received, but I don't think I can wait anymore," Aaron said, and Leslie felt him get off the bed for a minute. He looked over to see him stripping off the rest of his clothes before climbing back up on the bed and pressing against him.

Leslie whimpered a bit as he teased him with the tip, barely pressing into him and pulling back. It was torture, to be honest. Finally, he just snapped his hips forward and buried himself into the hilt. Leslie nearly screamed as he tried to keep himself from coming right then.

"The walls are thick, but they aren't that thick. You keep it up, my neighbors are gonna hear you, and those sounds belong to me alone," Aaron growled into his ear as he began working back and forth into him.

He continued his torturously slow pace for a while, and Leslie hoped that he had a new set of sheets because he knew this one was getting soaked already and he hadn't even come yet. Finally, Aaron seemed to have tired of tormenting Leslie slowly, and he sped up, hands and nails digging into his hips as he held onto him. It didn't take long for Leslie to start moaning as quietly as he could because he was at the right angle to rub against his prostate with each thrust.

"You're such a slut for this, you know that?" Aaron said in that same husky sounding voice that sent shivers down Leslie's spine. "I could fuck you every day and you'd never get tired of it, huh?"

Leslie had no answer for him; he was too far gone at the moment in his own world of sensation. He felt his orgasm rushing toward him, sending sensations throughout his body as the energy of Aaron's motion seemed to take over. Before he could say anything else, it hit him harder than he expected. He guessed that all the teasing and everything had made it like that. It didn't take but a few thrusts into him until Aaron came, slowing as he came to an end.

Aaron pulled out, and Leslie collapsed to the bed, wincing at the dampness underneath him. A second later, though, Aaron was wiping tear tracks from his face with a warm washcloth, then cleaning off his stomach and the bed. He put a towel over the wet place and climbed in beside Leslie, pulling him into his arms securely. Leslie was cold suddenly and started to shiver.

"You okay now?" Aaron asked, pulling the comforter up and over them both.

"Just a little cold," he answered, tightening his grip on Aaron's body.

"You seemed to like it," he continued, reaching up and running a hand through Leslie's hair.

"Yeah, is that weird?" he asked, nuzzling into Aaron's neck a little more.

Aaron snorted. "If the weirdest thing we ever do is a little spanking with a belt, I think we're pretty tame compared to other people."

"It's really okay to like that sort of thing?" Leslie was a little worried.

"Will you quit worrying?" Aaron sighed. "Ya were so worried about coming out in front of your friends, and you saw that worked out fine. So, this is fine too."

Leslie nodded, feeling suddenly very sleepy. "Okay, I think I love you; you know that?"

Aaron stiffened and Leslie wondered if he should have said anything. "You what?"

"I'm sorry, I didn't mean to..."

"No, no, don't apologize. I think I might just love you, too," Aaron whispered and kissed the top of his head.

Leslie fell asleep in Aaron's arms and Aaron soon followed him. Together, they'd spent their first New Year's together, and the night had led to things they hadn't expected.

# Stray Cat Chronicles
## Part Four

# They Stray Hearts

"You don't need to go through all that trouble. It's just Valentine's Day," Leslie said as he clutched his books to his chest. Valentine's day was the day after tomorrow.

"But it's our first Valentine's Day! Don't ya think we should do something?" Aaron asked, resisting the urge to reach out and grab Leslie's ass right then. It was a terribly strong urge because he was in a new pair of jeans that were kind of tight on him.

Leslie sighed, looking at Aaron with an exasperated expression. "Alright, alright. We can do something, I guess, if it'll make you happy."

"That's more like it!" Aaron said as they came into the building.

As usual, since they'd come "out" as a couple, things had gotten interesting. There were whispered conversations that they would catch snippets of now and then, and people would sometimes look at them strangely. Leslie always felt like he was on display or something, where Aaron would just grin and grab Leslie to him even tighter as if to show off for them.

Aaron didn't seem to mind those things in the least. When they were alone, Leslie would voice his concerns over the whole situation, and Aaron would find every way to minimize Leslie's fears on the issue. Especially since they now lived together. Of course, it made explaining the one bedroom place a little bit easier now that people knew they were a couple.

"We should go out for a nice dinner and a movie?" Aaron queried as they came into the main building on campus.

Leslie hesitated a tad too long before he answered. "Ah, all the places are going to be full of people. After all, it's Valentine's day, so dinner probably wouldn't be the best idea..."

Aaron arched a brow at him. "Why don't ya wanna go out to eat?"

Leslie stopped and looked at him. "We've got plenty to eat at home. And I know what I'm eating there," he said, the last a little lower than the first.

"But it's a special night. We should do something special for it!" he said, and Leslie looked around to see that people were looking at them.

"We'll talk about it after class, okay?" Leslie sighed and turned around to go to his class.

Aaron watched him go and wondered what that was all about. He shook it away and headed off to his own class and didn't think about it much more. He had his classes to worry about. Today he had one of his more interesting professors, so it made it easy to get lost in his classwork for the day. After his last class, he headed over to the student center to pick Leslie up so they could head home. He found him, as usual, sitting in the far corner at a table with his head buried in a book.

"Heya," Aaron said as he sat down across from him.

Leslie looked up, and once again, Aaron thought his face looked thinner. He frowned and noticed that there were no food wrappers on the table.

"Hey there. How was class?" Leslie asked, putting his legs down and closing his book.

"Good, good. Want me to grab you something from the food court? I'm starving," he said.

"Nah, I'm good. I'm not hungry," he said, smiling a little. "You go ahead, though."

Aaron frowned and stood up, heading over to the food area. He found himself a sub sandwich and chips with a soda. He saw they had those big cookies that were freshly baked, so he picked up a chocolate chip one, knowing they were Leslie's favorite. It was big enough to split between them even if he wasn't hungry. He left with the tray and sat back down, seeing Leslie had returned to reading while he waited.

"Look what I got," he said and slid the wrapped cookie across the table. "They're just made today. Thought we could split it."

Leslie stared at it for a second then looked at Aaron. "I don't know. I've been trying to cut down on sweets lately."

Aaron looked at him for a minute. "Cut down on sweets? You hardly eat anything lately."

"That's not true. I have to keep in shape for swimming." Leslie pushed the cookie back over at him.

"In shape?" Aaron asked as he started eating his sandwich while they talked. "Yer in shape! And if ya don't eat enough, yer gonna be outta shape more!"

"Do you have any idea how many calories are in something like that?" Leslie asked, looking at him with an extremely serious expression.

"No, and it's damn weird that you do," Aaron snapped.

"It's weird that I'm looking out for my weight?" Leslie narrowed his eyes at Aaron.

"Yes, because ya don't need to be! I can feel your ribs easy these days. I don't think you need to worry on yer weight that much!" Aaron said with a bit of exasperation.

Leslie sniffed and crossed his arms over his chest in a huff. "You have no idea what it's like."

"What? No idea what's like?" Aaron asked, pausing to drink his soda.

"To have to watch your weight! To have to make sure you don't gain any! To make sure that the numbers keep going down!" he said, staring at the table in front of him.

"Keep going down? Leslie, are you trying to lose more weight?" he asked, frowning at him now.

Leslie looked at him with a wide-eyed expression for a second and Aaron knew the answer to his question. "Why would you be trying to lose even more weight? Yer gettin' too thin as it is!"

"You don't understand," he said quietly, and Aaron just wanted to smack him across the face and snap him out of this line of thinking.

"I'm tryin' to!" Aaron said, sighing deeply.

"I just..." Leslie started, then just stopped. "Look, you'll never get it, alright? You can't. You eat whatever you want and never gain anything. You have always had a good metabolism and don't seem to have to worry about it slowing down. I do. I never had to worry about weight as a kid, but as I've gotten to my twenties, it's become obvious that it simply isn't the case."

"Leslie, you don't gain weight. I've been with ya nearly a year now, and you've been thin as a rail since I've known ya!" Aaron tried.

"Well, you don't know everything about me, now do you?" Leslie snapped, crossing his arms in a huff.

"I know enough to know that yer in perfectly fine shape and don't need to be losing any more weight!" Aaron was growing exasperated with Leslie's insistence that his weight was somehow a problem. It was ridiculous for him to be worried so much about it.

"You know what, I'm tired of talking since you aren't listening," he said, standing up. "I'm staying with Micah tonight," he said and stalked off, leaving Aaron watching after him.

"Well, fuck," Aaron whispered as he stared at the cookie where it still lay on the table.

Leslie was so angry at Aaron, unreasonably so, actually. For whatever reason, the conversation had tripped a nerve that Leslie didn't even know he had. He pulled out his phone and called Micah.

"Hey, Leslie," she answered cheerily.

"Can you pick me up at the school and let me sleep on your couch tonight?" he asked as he slowed down to a stop near the front of the building. "And maybe longer?"

There was a long pause. "Leslie, are you and Aaron fighting already?"

"Just a stupid argument," Leslie admitted, knowing that to anyone else it would seem trivial and stupid.

"You guys just moved in together last month, Leslie!" she said with obvious exasperation.

"It's not like we're breaking up or anything," Leslie said. "I just need a couple days away from him, that's all."

"That's not a good sign this early in your relationship," Micah told him.

"We've been dating almost a year, just no one knew about it. Except maybe the guys in swim class, I think they might have known what happened in the locker room..."

"The locker room? Really?" she said, sounding surprised.

"It was when we got together," he said, sighing. "It was really dumb, and we could've been caught, but we got lucky," he admitted.

"Oh, Leslie. I'll be there in ten. Out front?" she asked.

"Yeah," he said, looking out the door. "I'm already there."

"Okay, see you soon," she said before she hung up.

Leslie adjusted his bag and sighed. Why was he so mad, though? It was just a stupid cookie. He supposed he could have eaten the dumb cookie and made Aaron happy, then he could have got rid of it later… He really didn't want to resort to throwing up, though. He knew he could seriously mess up his teeth that way. But it was getting to the point that Aaron was noticing, and he couldn't hide it from him when they lived together. He saw Micah pull in in her little car. He walked out and got in sullenly.

"Well, you look terrible," she said as she took off again.

Leslie heard his phone ping and he gritted his teeth. He wasn't going to answer him right now because he was going to snap at him, and he knew it. "Thanks, Micah, I appreciate it," he muttered.

"I'm just being honest," she said as they headed to her house. "You've been looking bad lately. Have you been sick?"

"No, I'm fine," he said, staring out the side window.

They pulled into her house, and he got out clutching his bag. Was it really that noticeable? He swallowed hard as they came into the house.

"Yo, Micah, that you?" he heard.

"Yes, Aiden. Leslie's with me," she said as she shut the door behind them.

"Hey man," Aiden said as he came to the door. "What're you doing here?"

"He got in a fight with Aaron," Micah said before Leslie could say anything.

"It's not that big of a deal," Leslie said with a sigh.

"Not that much of a big deal? It's almost Valentine's Day! What the hell are ya fighting over two days before the big V-day?" Aiden said, scrunching his brow at Leslie.

"Just something stupid," he muttered and walked past him to the living room, hearing his phone go off again in his pocket.

"Well, it can't be that stupid if you didn't want to go home with him," Micah pointed out and crossed her arms over her chest as she came into the living room.

"It was over a cookie," he muttered as he flopped onto the sofa.

"A cookie?" Aiden said, dropping down into the chair next to him. Micah came up and leaned onto the arm of it.

"He got this stupid cookie and wanted to share it with me, and I didn't want it, and he didn't understand why, and he wanted to go to dinner on Valentine's Day and I didn't want to and so he got mad," he rambled out.

Aiden and Micah exchanged a glance. "Why in the world wouldn't you want to go to dinner?" she asked.

He sighed, chewing his thumbnail for a second. "I've just been trying really hard to stay in shape with swimming because I want to try out for the team this summer. So, I've been avoiding anything sweet, and he doesn't get it," he said slowly.

"I don't think you have anything to worry about," Aiden said with an arched brow. "Yer in fine shape and ya swim every afternoon, and sometimes every morning."

"It's not good enough, though," he said with a sigh.

Micah tilted her head to the side and looked at him for a minute. "Leslie, are you trying to keep in shape, or are you trying to control what you eat?"

He looked up, eyes darting between Aiden and Micah. "Both, I guess," he said, frowning. "Look, I got homework to do. Can we talk about this later?" he asked.

"Yeah, sure," Micah said, standing up. "I'll go get the spare linens so you can sleep here."

"Thanks," he told her as he rummaged in his bag.

That evening, Aiden and Micah ordered pizza and Leslie managed to convince them he wasn't hungry because he was still upset over the argument he had with Aaron. He thought if he had to, he could eat some of it, but he really didn't want to. He ended up falling asleep without looking at his messages at all, completely ignoring them.

The next morning, he woke up before Aiden and Micah and went to sit in the dining room with his phone. He opened up his text messages to see he had several from Aaron, as he expected.

Come on home. We can talk.

I know I'm shit at trying to understand sometimes, but I'm trying.

I miss you.

The bed feels empty without you here.

Please text me back and let me know you're ok.

Leslie sighed, putting down the phone. He nearly jumped out of his skin when Micah touched his shoulder.

"Sorry," she said as she sat down across from him.

"It's okay," he said, playing with the phone between his hands.

"Come on, Leslie, what's really going on?" she asked.

"What do you mean?" he frowned, looking over at her.

Micah stared at him for a minute. "You're mad because Aaron is concerned over your eating habits. That means there's something to be concerned about."

He swallowed and tried not to look at her. "No, it's just a stupid fight."

"No, it's not, Leslie." She obviously didn't believe him.

"M-maybe I've been keeping track of what I eat," he said finally.

She still stared at him. "Keeping track of what you eat?" she repeated.

He nodded. "I gave myself a set amount of calories to eat every day, and I keep to it or less," he said.

"How many calories, Leslie?" she asked.

"It doesn't matter," he tried, but he still didn't look at her.

She reached over the table and grabbed one of his hands. "Leslie, how many?"

He finally looked up at her, eyes a little wide. "It's enough, okay?" he said.

"Leslie..." she started but he stood up.

"I've gotta go by the apartment and change clothes," he said. "Then I've got class. I can call a cab if you're not able to take me."

She sighed and nodded. "I can take you."

Micah left the issue alone, but Leslie knew that she was worried about it now. Just what he needed, his other friends starting in on him too. He knew they meant well, but he needed them to just leave it alone. He knew what he was doing. He'd looked up stuff online about dieting and exercise and he knew the only way to lose weight was to create a calorie deficit. To do that, he had to restrict the amount of calories he took in. He had to get down to 125 pounds or less. He was only down to 134 since he started tracking his intake. It was better than the original weight of 145, but it wasn't good enough. He had to lower his weight more before it was time to try out for the swim team.

Leslie didn't realize how much time he was spending obsessing over the numbers. He was tracking everything and restricting himself to only eating what he knew exactly how many calories it had. He knew that muscle weighed more than fat, so he was avoiding weights, instead sticking to swimming and aerobic exercises when he was working out.

He realized they were at the apartment complex, and he got out of the car without a word to Micah. He knew she'd wait for him, however long he took. He got inside and changed clothes quickly, pausing to look in the mirror on the back of the closet door. What if they were right? What if what he was doing was bad? He shook his head and left. No, he knew what he was doing. He was fine.

Micah stared as he got back in the car but didn't say anything. He was glad of that because he didn't really feel like talking any more. He sighed and heard his phone ping again. He swallowed and looked at it.

Please talk to me.

Leslie sighed as his finger hesitated over the screen. Finally, he sent a message. I'm fine.

A few tense seconds passed, and another message came through. I don't want to fight. Come home tonight.

He realized they'd stopped, and Micah was staring at him. "What?" he asked.

"He's just worried about you," she said, giving him a small smile. "So am I."

"I'm fine," he told her, putting his phone away.

"No, you're not, Leslie. Please, this isn't good for you, whatever you're doing. You've got to understand that, don't you?" she reached out and put a hand on his shoulder.

"Look, I gotta go," he said, reaching for the door. "I'll call you later. I don't know if I'm going home or not tonight yet."

She nodded. "Just let me know," she said as he left the car.

He was just fine.

Aaron could barely concentrate in class, he was so worried about the situation with Leslie. He found himself checking his phone every few seconds to see if he'd sent him another message. At least he'd finally answered him, so that was a good thing. Now, he just had to get him to come home tonight.

"Are you with us, Mr. Clark?" the professor asked, bringing him out of his reverie.

"Ah, yes, sir," he said, looking up at him. "Sorry, personal issue on my mind."

"Well, let's leave the personal issues outside of class, shall we?"

"Yeah, sorry," he answered, watching him turn back to the white board and continue to teach.

By the time his classes were done, Aaron just felt empty, like he'd given out everything he had, and he had no more to give. He went to the food court and had another sub sandwich, hoping that Leslie would show up there like usual. He didn't. He jerked when he felt his phone vibrate. He pulled it out and found a number he didn't know texted him.

Aaron, this is Micah, Leslie's friend. Aiden had your number, I guess Leslie gave it to him.

Yeah, that's cool. What's up? He had no idea what she was messaging him about. He rarely talked to her since the New Year's party.

I'm worried about Leslie. He said something that worries me, about restricting his food intake. Have you noticed it?

He frowned at the screen, recalling how many times he had to encourage him to eat just since Christmas. It had started a couple months before, but he wasn't living with him at that point. He just thought that Leslie was being picky about what he ate because of swimming.

Something like that. Do you think it's a problem?

How often do you see him eat anything? He didn't eat the entire time he was here though we tried to get him to.

Aaron frowned. He hadn't eaten before either. That and he drank an awful lot of water at home. Yeah, I see what you mean. What do I do?

I don't know. He won't listen to me.

He sighed, not sure how to deal with the situation at all. I'll try to talk to him again.

He exited the messaging app and went to the internet. He started searching for the things that Leslie was doing, and he sat staring at the possible answer for a second, not sure if he was right. That was a thing girls did, wasn't it? Guys didn't do that. But he found out it wasn't true. It could happen to anyone, it seemed. He put down the phone and worried still more. What should he do?

When he didn't get anything from Leslie by five, he decided to go home. He was a little depressed because the next day was Valentine's Day, and he'd planned to have a special day with him. He wondered if that was possible anymore. He'd almost fallen asleep when he felt his phone buzz in his hand, waking him up.

I'm coming home.

Aaron sat up, half dressed and half asleep. He checked the time and saw it was just after midnight. What in the world was

Leslie doing awake at this hour, let alone getting someone to bring him home? He heard the door a few minutes later and Leslie came into the bedroom.

"You're back." He didn't know what else to say, honestly.

"Yeah," he said as he came and sat down on the side of the bed.

"I'm sorry, for whatever I did. I still don't understand, but I'm trying to," Aaron said and sat down in the bed.

Leslie was quiet for a minute. "There's something wrong with me."

"There's nothing wrong with you," he said, reaching out and putting a hand on his leg.

For a second, it was quiet. "I-I couldn't sleep. I tried, but I kept thinking about things, and I couldn't stay away anymore. Micah was up late studying anyway, so she brought me home."

"I'm glad you came home. I missed you," Aaron told him as he slid his hand to squeeze at his knee.

"Micah's worried about me now," he sighed. "I worried you, too."

"It's okay, I'm supposed to worry about ya," Aaron said.

"Yeah. I don't know what to do, Aaron. What am I supposed to do?" Leslie said and turned toward him on the bed.

"You do what you need to do. You get some help with it, that's what you do," Aaron moved and cupped his face. Leslie turned into Aaron's hand and closed his eyes. "Let's think about that some more tomorrow. For now, it's late."

"Yeah, I guess so." He still didn't open his eyes though. "It's already Valentine's Day, you know," he added.

"Yeah, it sure is," Aaron answered, sweeping his thumb over Leslie's lips. "You want your present now, or later?"

Leslie's eyes opened. "Present?" he asked. "But I didn't get you a present!"

"Ah, but my present is really for both of us. Besides, there's only one present I want," he said as a mischievous smirk spread across his face.

"Aaron..." Leslie said, frowning a little. "I thought you were tired?"

"Nah, not anymore. Thinkin' about your present got me all worked up. It ain't somethin' you can show anyone else though," he said with the smirk still firmly plastered to his face.

"What'd you buy?" Leslie asked suspiciously.

Aaron winked at him and slid off the bed, going over to the closet to get a bag. The bag was a red gift bag with a purple heart on the front, and for some reason, Leslie thought that the logo looked familiar. Then it hit him. It was the local sex shop.

"You went there?" Leslie asked, wide eyed.

"Uh huh," Aaron said, handing the bag to him. "Go on, see what's inside."

Leslie hesitated but looked inside. He pulled out a box. It was an assortment pack of various toys. Leslie's face reddened immediately.

"I already cleaned 'em all, and put batteries in the ones that need them," Aaron said, standing over Leslie with the smirk still plastered to his face. "Boy, were they busy. I was lucky to get something."

"I can't... You bought this?" Leslie finally stammered, looking up at him with wide eyes. "Like, you walked into that store and bought this?"

"Ain't that big of a deal. I wasn't the only one buying fun stuff. I also got some lube to try that the girl at the counter said was a lot better than the stuff we get at the grocery store," Aaron said, reaching in the bag and pulling out a bottle.

"You talked to someone, even?" Leslie asked, still red in the face.

"She was real nice when I told her I'd never been in there before. She suggested this as something to try for first timers with toys because it has different things in it to try out," he took the box from Leslie and opened it, pulling out the molded plastic with the toys in it.

"What do you do with them?" Leslie asked, staring at the various things.

"What do you think you do with them?" Aaron asked, dumping the whole of them on the bed in a pile.

Leslie picked up the thick vibrator and looked at Aaron. "But we've never done anything like this..."

"Gotta start somewhere. Whaddaya think about trying them out because I'm horny as hell just thinking about it," Aaron leaned forward and plucked the vibrator from his hand.

"Now?" Leslie said, cheeks still blushing redly.

"Uh huh," Aaron said, stepping forward and sliding a hand up the inside of Leslie's thigh to palm his crotch. "Yer already getting hard thinkin' about it, you little slut," he murmured, leaning in and kissing at his throat. "Come on, Leslie-babe, let's have some fun and tomorrow I'll take you out for a night doin' whatever ya want."

"Hah," Leslie breathed, baring his throat even more to Aaron's kisses and light bites.

"That's my boy," Aaron murmured and grabbed the bottom of Leslie's t-shirt, slipping it over his head to toss it aside. He was still in his jeans, but he wanted to play before he did anything else. "Come on, let's take this off, too."

Leslie wriggled a little as Aaron undid his jeans and shifted them down over his hips. Again, he noticed the weight that Leslie had lost, and he knew this was going to be a long talk come morning. But for now, he had other things in mind, like trying out every toy in that box before he was done. He stroked him a couple times as he realized he had gotten worked up as well. He reached over and grabbed a ring out of the pile and started working it down over Leslie's cock.

"What? What is that for?" Leslie stammered, hands flat beside him on the bed.

"Oh, it'll help you keep going longer," Aaron explained, taking a moment to stroke him again. Leslie let out a little moan that Aaron almost lost it at. "Come on, up in the bed," he said and helped Leslie lay down on his back.

"It's tight," he muttered, starting to reach for himself.

Aaron grabbed his hands and pulled out the two leather cuffs that were at the bottom of the bag. Leslie's eyes went a little wide as Aaron buckled them on his wrists. He checked to make sure he could get a finger underneath each of them, then pushed Leslie over onto his stomach. The cuffs had a clip that connected them to each other and he snapped it together behind his back.

"I'm not sure about this..." Leslie said as his fingers flexed for a minute.

"If it gets too much, just tell me, and I'll take them off," Aaron assured him as he leaned forward and began kissing down his spine.

Aaron reached over and grabbed the bottle of lube he'd bought. He popped it open and could smell the mint scent already. He looked down at Leslie's hands bound behind him and smirked. It was a nice sight, he thought to himself. He grabbed the vibrator first, coating it with the lube. He gently pushed Leslie's legs open more as he slipped the tip of it into him. He heard him make a little noise. Aaron was expecting to get a lot of different noises out of him before he was done. He slid it forward more and heard Leslie's breathing hitch a little.

"You okay?" he asked, pausing as he sat there.

"Yeah, just feels weird," he panted a little.

Aaron slid it forward a little more, then turned it onto the lowest setting. Leslie's legs twitched and he cried out suddenly. He could hear the sound to his voice as he slid the vibrator in deeper.

"Ngh!"

"Still okay?" Aaron asked, steadily pushing and pulling on the vibrator.

"Yes, my gods, yes, it feels... it feels... I don't know!" he gasped out finally.

Aaron reached underneath him and found him leaking profusely. "Hmm, it seems you like it. That ring helping?"

"Take it off so I can come, please!" he whined. "I need to!"

"Uh ah, not yet, my little slut. You can't come with a piece of plastic in yer ass. My dick is the only thing yer allowed to come on, understand?" he said and twisted the vibrator to a higher setting. The resulting cries made Aaron happy.

"Please!" he begged. "Just let me... I can't..."

"No, not yet, there's still more toys to play with," he said and slipped the vibrator out of him.

Leslie was panting against the sheets now, hands balled into tight fists at his back. Aaron picked up the beads and squeezed out a little lube onto them. There were six balls of increasing size, with the last one being about an inch in diameter. It was smaller than the width of the vibrator, but he had a feeling it would still do the job.

He slowly popped the first ball into him, which received a shuddering breath. Then he worked the next one into him, getting a lovely whimper from him for that one. Next, he worked the third and fourth ones in, feeling his body tense at the increasing size. By the time he popped the fifth and sixth one in, he could hear a steady moaning coming from him.

"You like that?" he asked, tugging at the base of the string of beads just enough to start to pull the bottom one out, then letting it go back in.

"It feels funny..." he said, ass wiggling attractively as he laid there trying desperately to be still.

"Hmm, I thought I could hold out, but I don't think I can wait much longer. Right now, I want to plunge my dick in your ass, and forget all these toys..." Aaron told him as he started to pull back on the beads. He watched them pop out one at a time, slowly, and he knew that Leslie was having trouble holding on.

"Oh, please, I'm gonna come," Leslie moaned as he tried to keep his voice down.

"Here, I'm gonna let you come," Aaron promised, reaching up and rolling Leslie to his back onto his hands. "But only so I can see you."

Leslie's eyes were damp, and he was panting harder. Aaron leaned over and locked his mouth on him, slowly exploring him with his tongue. He reached down and began working the cockring off him. Once he'd pulled it off, he tossed it in the pile with the other toys to be cleaned later. He could feel Leslie's legs tightening around him. He reached down and pulled himself free of his jeans, sliding up and into Leslie with little effort. It seemed the gal at the store was right, and there was a big difference in good lube.

"Let my arms go, please!" Leslie asked, tugging at his wrists.

"Alright, just a minute," Aaron said as he adjusted enough to pull Leslie up and reach the clip between the cuffs. It was easy to release, at least, he noticed as he freed Leslie's hands from each other.

Immediately, Leslie's arms went around his neck, and he let out a deep moan, gripping him tightly. Aaron put his hands around Leslie's back and slammed up into him where he was halfway sitting up on him. Leslie's head dropped back, and he made a noise deep in his throat.

"Ya can only come on my dick, understand that?" Aaron told him. "Good sluts do what they're told, don't they?"

"Yeah," Leslie breathed out, burying his head in Aaron's shoulder.

"Good," Aaron said and began thrusting hard into him, setting him in a series of steady moaning sounds.

He felt Leslie leaking between them at every thrust into his body. He was trying really hard to hold off, and Aaron could tell. He finally gripped his ass hard and rammed into him hard enough to set him onto his back. He reached up and ran a hand over Leslie's head. He couldn't decide which he liked better, hearing him beg or hearing him moan with release. Both were pretty wonderful things, in his opinion.

"Does my slut want to come?" he asked, leaning down and kissing his collarbone.

"Please!" he begged, legs flexing around Aaron.

"Hmm, how can I resist such a slutty demand?" Aaron asked and leaned up to kiss him, mouth seeking out Leslie's. "Come, then, come for me," he breathed into his ear.

Leslie's body immediately reacted, shaking and quivering in release. Aaron gritted his teeth as he felt Leslie's body clench him in the warmth of his body. He thrust down into him a couple more times and felt himself go over the edge, barely able to hold on as he clutched Leslie toward his body. He thrust shallowly into him a couple times before he fell to the side, legs still entangled.

He reached up and ran a hand through Leslie's damp hair. He was breathing deeply still. "Hmm, I think the toys were a success," he said with a smirk.

"Oh, my gods," Leslie said. "I thought I was never going to come," he said, smiling at Aaron now.

"Well, you know I won't make you wait forever," Aaron told him and leaned down to engage his mouth in a long, languid kiss.

They were quiet for a while and then Aaron sighed. "I think we're going to need a long talk."

"Yeah," Leslie said. "I guess so."

"You promise not to get mad over a cookie this time?" Aaron asked, propping himself up on his elbow and looking down into Leslie's face.

Leslie smiled. "I promise. That was really stupid," he said with a sigh.

"Nah, it isn't stupid, but we gotta figure this out. I can't watch you do this to yerself," Aaron said, snaking an arm over Leslie's chest.

Leslie swallowed hard. "Yeah, I know. I guess I thought I could control it, and I guess I can't."

"How long has this been going on?" Aaron rubbed a hand gently over his chest.

"I don't know. I think it started when I decided to start swim class, but it wasn't as bad then. I just got a little obsessed with making sure I didn't gain anything. Then it just went from there, and I wasn't eating every meal, and then I started counting the calories in everything and restricting what I ate, and..." he trailed off.

"It's okay, we'll work through it, okay? You can't do it on your own," Aaron told him softly.

Leslie turned and hugged him, wrapping his arms around Aaron's body. Aaron felt tears begin to wet his shoulder. He had no idea what kind of road they had ahead of them, but they'd make it, one way or another.

# Stray Cat Chronicles
## Part Five

## Strays Under the Stars

"A picnic under the stars?" Leslie asked curiously.

"Yeah, you've been doing so good lately with everything that I want to do something special. No real reason," Aaron responded as they came into their apartment.

It had been over a month since everything came out at Valentine's Day. They had talked a lot over the next week, and Leslie acknowledged he had a problem and needed to do something about it. It hadn't gotten any better, of course. Just knowing what the problem was didn't fix it. Aaron began keeping track of what Leslie ate, but for a different reason than he did. He also knew almost immediately when he was lying about eating something. Leslie had a hard time keeping it out of his face.

Aaron had insisted on Leslie sticking to a strict eating schedule. He still tried to put eating off, or tried to avoid it altogether, but Aaron wouldn't let him get away with it for long. It was a struggle to get him to stop counting the calories in everything that he ate, and Aaron knew he was still keeping track of it no matter what he said. He hadn't convinced him to go see a therapist yet, though. That was the one area Leslie hadn't budged. He claimed to not need anyone. Aaron thought differently, but he was going to give him a chance to work through things on his own before he insisted on outside help.

"I think you just want to have sex outside," Leslie said as he sat down on the bed and crossed his arms.

"Now, why would you say something like that?" he asked as he walked over and cupped his face.

"Everything with you leads to sex." Leslie arched a brow at him.

Aaron sighed and shook his head. "I'm not planning on having sex outside, if you must know. Now, when we get back home, I can't make any guarantees."

Leslie sighed. "I don't know," he muttered, looking away. Aaron could already see him mentally calculating what foods they were going to take to see if he'd eat.

"Look, we can invite Micah and Aiden and make a night of it. And didn't you say your friend Dominic finally asked the girl with the big boobs that likes you out?" Aaron asked, stroking his thumb across Leslie's chin.

Sighing, Leslie knew he couldn't say no to that face when he was asking like that. "Yeah, Dominic finally asked her. I guess he never asked her because he thought he would be getting between her and me, but when we got together, he decided that wouldn't be a problem anymore."

"See, there, wouldn't it be nice to go out for a nice evening with them? We haven't done anything like that before. And you've been doing a good job sticking to your food schedule," Aaron pointed out, standing up straight and putting his hands on his hips.

Leslie looked up at him and gave him a small smile. "If you really want to, I can ask Dominic and Micah if they're interested in doing something like that. I'm meeting Micah for a study session tomorrow afternoon after class. I can talk to her then and text Dominic."

Aaron leaned over and kissed his head and undressed to crawl into bed. It had been a busy day, and both of them were tired.

Aaron, though, worried as Leslie fell asleep in his arms. His fingers slid down his sides where his ribs were still too pronounced, and his hips where the bones jutted out a bit too much. He was scared, to be honest. He loved him too much to watch him destroy himself.

Leslie honestly forgot. It wasn't on purpose. He just forgot to eat before he left the apartment with Aaron. They'd gotten up late, both sleeping through the alarm on Aaron's phone. Luckily, Micah had called Leslie to make sure they were still on for studying that day, and he woke up. They weren't too late, so it was no harm, except of course, Leslie didn't have breakfast before he left. Even Aaron, being as rushed as he was, didn't think of it as they got out the door as quickly as possible.

Then, at lunch, he thought about eating. In fact, he had a text from Aaron reminding him that he needed to get lunch since they both missed breakfast. He had been about to do it, but then he got a text back from Dominic about the nighttime picnic, and it distracted him. So, he just didn't think about it at all. It wasn't really on purpose.

After he'd arranged everything with Dominic and Emily for the weekend, he just left to go meet Micah. She was to pick him up and they were going to study at her house. He was just so used to going without eating that it didn't really dawn on him that he'd completely skipped lunch now.

"Hey," he said as he dropped into her car. "How's it going?"

"Great. You bring your English books?" she asked as she pulled out of the parking lot.

"Of course. Hard to study without them," he said as he patted his bookbag.

"Aaron mind you taking off for the evening?"

"Nah, he was cool with it. Oh! That reminds me. Would you and Aiden be up for a night picnic Saturday night?" he asked, smiling at her.

She glanced over and shrugged. "I'll ask Aiden, but I don't think we're doing anything Saturday."

"Great, Dominic and Emily are coming too, so it would be a cool outing for everyone."

They pulled into the house and got out. It was then Leslie realized he'd forgotten to eat. He'd gotten back on a schedule lately, so messing with it was starting to become noticeable. He thought about saying something to Micah, but then figured they'd probably order pizza or something tonight, so it would be fine. He could wait until later to eat. He just wouldn't tell Aaron about it since he even went to the trouble of reminding him of it.

They set about studying their English work as soon as they got settled in around the table in the dining room. It was one of the only classes he shared with Micah, so they often studied together before big tests. This test was on imagery and meaning in poetry. Leslie liked it alright; he just needed a little extra help with it sometimes. It was a couple hours later when he needed to use the bathroom. He hadn't really drank anything today either, he realized. He was about to turn and say something to Micah when he stood up, but a wave of dizziness washed over him, and he felt the world fade out at the edges of his vision.

The next thing he knew he was on the floor looking up at Micah's concerned face. He blinked, feeling a bit fuzzy around the edges. "What happened?"

"Are you alright? You passed out!" she said, clinging to his arm.

He slowly sat up, shaking his head. "I haven't done that in a while," he muttered.

Micah heard him. "You've passed out before?" she asked, shock apparent in her voice.

He winced, not meaning to have said something about it. "It's just low blood sugar. I haven't eaten today, and—"

"You haven't eaten today?" she snapped at him.

"I got busy! I missed breakfast because we were late, and then Dominic texted me, and then it was time to meet with you, and I just didn't think of it..." he trailed off, looking at her, a little embarrassed.

Aaron had talked to Micah about what was going on, he knew. But he didn't know how much she knew about it. She certainly wouldn't know that Aaron had been keeping him on an eating schedule for the last couple of weeks.

"Well, stand up. You're going to eat something now," she said as she stood up herself.

"Alright, let me go to the bathroom first," he said as he got to his feet a little shakily.

He stopped and stared at his face in the mirror and wondered if it was really as bad as Aaron was making it out to be. Surely losing a little weight wouldn't hurt him. But passing out was kind of scary, he guessed. He'd never passed out in front of anyone else before. He shook his head and ran his hands through the dark locks on his head. He was just fine. It was just one time he forgot to eat. It wasn't that big of a deal.

When he came out, Micah was holding an apple out to him. "Here, eat this now, and we're ordering something in for later."

"It's really not that much of a problem. I'm fine now," he said, taking the apple tentatively.

Despite his promise to Aaron, he really didn't feel like eating it. His brain automatically calculated that the average apple had around ninety-five calories give or take. He looked at it for a minute and then saw that Micah was staring at him. He sighed, knowing if he didn't eat it, she was going to be upset with him. He swallowed and took a bite out of it. She nodded to him once and led him back to the table.

"This is a bigger problem than you make it out to be, Leslie," she pointed out as she stared across the table at him.

"It's really not," he tried.

"Aaron said you were still trying to restrict your calories," she commented, watching him as he ate the apple slowly.

He gave an exasperated sigh. "It's not as bad as it was. I'm not doing it as much as I was before, so I'm getting better about it. Besides, there's no harm in watching out how many calories I eat."

"There's a difference between watching how many calories you eat and nearly going without eating at all," she said, crossing her arms over her chest.

"It was just an accident today, that's all," he said, putting the apple core down on the table.

"Leslie, it's never just an accident. You've set yourself up so you have an excuse not to eat when you can, haven't you?" She gave him a hard look.

"I eat three times a day!" He frowned at her and crossed his own arms over his chest. He didn't really want to discuss this any further, but he knew she wasn't going to let it go easily.

She arched a brow at him. "Oh, and what do you eat?"

He looked at her and knew if he lied, she'd know, just like Aaron always did. "I eat enough."

"You're not telling the whole truth at all, and you know it. You're still eating the absolute minimum to keep Aaron off your case, aren't you?" she narrowed her eyes at him.

He glanced away from her face and bit down on his lip for a minute. "I eat something before I leave the apartment with Aaron. Something light because I don't like to eat a lot in the morning. Then I eat something at the school, and I have something at home when I get back there in the evening."

"But what are you eating, Leslie?" she asked, still watching him carefully.

"Does it matter?" he asked, looking at her sharply.

"Yes!" she exclaimed. "It matters a lot, Leslie. You're trying to keep Aaron from getting mad at you, so you're eating something, but it isn't enough, whatever it is," she told him.

He leaned forward and put his elbows on the table and his head in his hands. "I don't know, Micah. I'm doing everything I can to make it go away! I am! But... It's just not working right."

"That's because you need some help, idiot," she groused with a shake of her head. "You need to see a therapist or something."

He looked at her and shook his head. "I don't need a therapist. Aaron's been trying to get me to see one, too, but I don't need one."

"Obviously, you're struggling with this, Leslie. Why not get some outside help?" she asked, putting a hand gently on his shoulder.

"I don't know. I just... I don't want to talk to some stranger, okay?" he said, sitting back up and staring up at the ceiling. "I can do this by myself."

"You can't, Leslie. You've been trying for over a month and you're not doing better than before. In fact, I think you've lost even more weight," she huffed a sigh as she glared at him.

"Only five pounds," he muttered, but cut his eyes up at her.

"Five pounds? Leslie! You're supposed to be gaining back the extra weight you've lost. You don't need to be losing anymore!" she said, squeezing his shoulder with a frown.

"I can't help it, Micah! I'm trying, I really am!" he said, starting to get annoyed with her now. "Look, can we just study? I'm tired of talking about it."

She looked at him for a minute, then shook her head. "Yeah, I guess. But you're eating when I order pizza tonight, got it?"

"I will. I promise."

Of course, when the pizza did come, Leslie managed one piece before he was trying to say he was full and didn't need anymore. All he could think about was how many calories were in each piece of pizza. It was only a pepperoni and cheese pizza, but still. He knew that each piece was about three hundred calories. Even though he'd only eaten an apple so far, he still couldn't get past the idea of eating nearly six hundred calories if he ate two pieces of pizza.

"Stop thinking so hard and eat another piece, Leslie," Micah said with a sigh.

Leslie looked at her. "No, I'm really okay with one."

"That's not enough. I ate more than you and I'm half your size. You're thinking about the calories in it, aren't you?" she asked, crossing her arms at him and frowning.

"Well, it's a lot at one sitting, you know. At one time. I mean, it's half a day's calories just in a couple pieces, and—"

"Half a day's calories?" she interrupted. "Leslie, you haven't even eaten the other half of your calories for the day yet."

He looked at her again, swallowing. "Look, it's enough. I don't want any more."

"Fine, but I'm telling Aaron you passed out today," she said, standing up and taking the pizza box to the fridge.

"No!" he nearly shouted as he stood up to follow her. "You don't have to do that!"

"Leslie, he should know something like that," she told him as she came back.

"Please, he doesn't have to know!" he tried.

Micah shook her head as she went toward the door to grab her jacket. "Come on, I'm taking you home. It's late," she said.

Leslie grabbed his bag and went to the car with her. He was sullen all the way back to the apartment, staring out the side window at the world moving past them. He knew that she meant well, but he just didn't need any help. And now Aaron was going to be mad at him. He sighed as they pulled into the complex and looked at her.

"I won't tell him," she said, looking at him. "As long as you promise not to let it happen again."

"I promise, alright?" he said, smiling at her, glad that she wasn't going to tell Aaron after all.

She shook her head as he got out of the car to go in. He waved at her and headed up the stairs to the apartment.

Aaron had a feeling Leslie wasn't telling him something. It was just a niggling at his brain, but he knew Leslie by now, and he knew that guilty face he got every once in a while. He also knew that he couldn't keep it from him forever and he'd find out what he was hiding. By the time Saturday came, he was still sure there was something he wasn't telling him.

"Are we meeting everyone at the camping ground?" Leslie asked as he packed some water bottles into his bag.

"Yeah, Aiden texted me and said they were picking up Emily and Dominic on the way, so they'll come together," he said as he slipped his phone into his pocket. "You think you got enough?"

Leslie looked. He'd stuck five bottles of water in the bag. "Oh, I guess I don't need that many," he said, flushing a bit. He pulled out one. "Just four, two for you and two for me," he said and zipped it up. "Okay I'm ready."

Smiling, Aaron reached for his hand. Leslie grabbed it and squeezed. "Alright, let's go."

They drove to the campground where they were meeting up. It wasn't very far out of town, but it was far enough to be out of the city lights, so the sky was rather clear and bright.

"It's so weird to see so many stars," Leslie said as he got out of the car and looked up. It was already past eight, so they were coming out.

They heard another car coming into the parking lot and saw Aiden's SUV with the others. Leslie waved and watched as everyone got out of the car.

"Yo," Aiden said as he got out and went around to the back to grab the supplies.

"Need some help?" Aaron asked as he walked around the end of the car.

"Sure, here," he said as he handed him a bag of chips.

Leslie went over to the clearing with Emily and Micah. Micah had a large blanket that they were going to spread out on the ground. He helped her get it all situated and by then, Aiden, Aaron, and Dominic came over with the rest of the stuff for the picnic.

After they got everything passed out and settled in, everyone had a sandwich that Micah had made, and some tea cakes that Emily had baked. There was some trepidation about that, because Emily had some decidedly odd tastes, but these were strawberry and cream flavored. They chatted about school and how things were going.

"So, have you and Emily gone on any fun dates yet?" Micah asked Dominic as she ate her teacake.

Dominic adjusted his glasses up his nose. "We've gone out to eat a couple times, but nowhere really special yet. With school and all, it's been too busy."

"Dominic took me to a really nice little café, though," Emily said with a broad smile. "It was such a cute little place."

Leslie was still picking at his sandwich when Aaron glanced over at him. He frowned and reached over and squeezed his thigh. He looked up, knowing he'd been caught avoiding eating.

"Leslie, you promised me you were going to eat tonight," Micah reminded him.

Emily looked over at him. "Haven't you been eating, Leslie?"

"He's been trying not to, but we're working on it, aren't we Leslie?" Aaron said and looked at him.

"I'm just not very hungry," he said, looking down and away from Aaron.

Aaron growled under his breath. "Leslie. You didn't eat much at lunch because you promised to eat tonight."

"I just don't want to, alright?" he said and sat the half-eaten sandwich down on the paper plate.

"Leslie," Micah said, narrowing her eyes at him. "You are making a lot of promises and not keeping them. You're going to pass out again."

"Again?" Aaron said, turning to him with a scowl.

The moment she said it, Aaron knew he'd figured out what he was hiding from him. His shoulders tensed and he just stared down at his hands, avoiding Aaron's gaze. "It wasn't that bad," he muttered.

Aaron sighed and rubbed his head. "Leslie. You can't keep this up. You're going to seriously damage yourself at this rate."

"He also said he's still lost weight again," Micah said, glaring at Leslie.

"Hey!" Leslie said and looked at her sharply. "Only a little!"

"You're supposed to be gaining back the weight you lost," Aaron reminded him.

Dominic looked over at him. "Leslie, it isn't good for you to lose weight. You have been looking poor lately, I suppose that's why."

"Why would you want to lose weight?" Emily asked, frowning now. "You're so thin as it is, and you swim all the time!"

Aaron knew Leslie felt on the spot because everyone was looking at him, wanting answers out of him. Aiden hadn't said anything, but he was watching him just the same as everyone else. Leslie finally huffed and stood up, walking away from the group toward the trees. Aaron looked at the others and sighed.

They let Leslie have some space as he stood over by the grove and ignored them as they continued to talk about other things for a little while longer. Finally, Micah and Aiden started packing up everything, leaving Leslie's tea cake for him.

"Leslie, we're going to go," Micah yelled over at him.

He waved at her over his shoulder but didn't turn around. Aaron sighed and looked at her. "I'll see if I can talk to him."

"Alright, don't forget to bring the blanket home, okay?" she said as she headed over to the car with the others.

Aaron watched them leave, then went over where Leslie was standing and snaked his arms around his waist.

"Ya gonna stay mad?" he asked.

"Yes," Leslie said but didn't move Aaron's hands where they rested on his hips.

"Come on, now," Aaron told him and turned him around to face him. "Don't be like this."

"I'll be however I want," he said, meeting Aaron's eyes.

"Tell you what, come eat the tea cake that Emily made, and then we'll head home," he said, trying to smile a little at him.

Leslie snorted. "I don't want to eat anything right now. I'm still mad."

"Please? For me?" Aaron gave him as much of an innocent face as someone as rough as Aaron could.

"If I do, will you leave it alone?" he grumbled, finally reaching his arms around Aaron's neck.

Aaron nodded. "For tonight. But we're going to talk some more in the morning. You need to see someone, and I'm not going to take no for an answer," Aaron told him.

Leslie nodded slowly. "I'm sorry I'm not strong enough to do this alone," he whispered.

"Don't. Leslie-babe, you gotta know it's not just you alone. I'm here, and so are your other friends. Everyone wants to see you happy and healthy. And what you're doing isn't healthy at all, but it isn't your fault, and you can get help from a professional." Aaron threaded his fingers through his hair thoughtfully.

"But I don't want to talk to a stranger," he said, sighing in defeat.

"I know, but you need to. We'll find someone, and you can go see them. If you don't like them, you don't have to go back, okay? And we'll keep looking for someone you do like until we find a good match," Aaron said gently, smiling at him.

He nodded slowly and Aaron kissed his forehead. Leslie turned his face up and met his lips. It started as a chaste kiss, but it soon deepened into more than that, both of them panting for breath when they broke apart.

"Ah, hell. I'm not waiting until we get home," Aaron muttered and began pulling Leslie over to the blanket again.

Leslie, a little shocked, was pulled along until they were standing on the blanket together. "Wait, here?" he asked, eyes widening a little.

"I brought the lube. I put it in your bag," Aaron said, turning toward the bag and fishing out the small bottle from the bag and slipping it into his pocket.

"You planned this!" Leslie exclaimed, glaring at him. "You said you didn't want to have sex outside!"

"Sorry, I just can't wait, come here, it won't be that bad. The ground's not too hard here on the blanket. And we can wash the blanket before we give it back to Micah," he said and reached for the button on Leslie's jeans.

Leslie stammered, "But what if someone sees us!"

"It's almost midnight, and the stars are the only witnesses out here now," he said, quickly sliding the pants off Leslie's hips.

Leslie looked like he wanted to argue, but Aaron leaned down and engaged him in another kiss that quickly turned heated again, and as he brushed up against him, he could feel that he'd definitely acquired his interest. He slipped a hand down over the outside of his shorts and palmed him through them.

"Look at you, my good slut. Already getting all wet for me," he muttered. At his words he felt him twitch and he grinned again.

Leslie whimpered a little but moved to put his arms around Aaron's neck and kissed him again. This time, as they kissed, Aaron slid the shorts over his hips to let them fall down his legs.

"It's cold out here," Leslie mumbled against his lips. "I'm going to freeze."

"Just a minute, and I'll warm ya up," Aaron said and reached behind to squeeze his ass with both hands.

Leslie fell into him, and Aaron was next lowering them to the ground slowly. He was already hard in his own jeans and wanted nothing more than to turn Leslie around and slam his cock into him as hard as he could. But he'd be a little considerate of him, and at least prepare him with the lube before he fucked him.

He undid his jeans and Leslie moved around to look up at him with those sparkling brown eyes and he growled. "Down," he instructed, and Leslie reached over and pulled him free of the pants.

Leslie cut his eyes up at him as he leaned down and took him into his mouth slowly. Aaron growled low in his throat again and watched as he bobbed his head down on him, taking him down about halfway. It was good, but he could do better, Aaron knew. He buried both hands in his hair and shoved his head down hard until he felt his cock slide down into his throat. He heard him sputter a bit, and felt his throat constrict on him.

"Good, good slut. You like my cock?" he muttered as he dragged his head up and off of him.

Leslie looked at him with watering eyes and a panting, wet mouth. It was all too much as Aaron shoved him back down again. He waited until he started to push back harder against him and let him come up and cough a few times.

"Turn around here," he told him, and Leslie turned away from him, dropping to his elbows and knees.

Aaron kicked his legs wider and slipped his cock up and down the outside of him. He felt him shiver a little and he fished the bottle of lube out of his pocket. He squeezed some out and coated himself with it, the tingly mint smell filling the air around them. He tossed the bottle to the side and then licked his lips as he stared for a minute at his ass. He smirked and drew back a hand and slapped him hard enough to make him yell out.

"What're you doing?" Leslie gasped.

"Having a little fun, be still," Aaron muttered as he drew back again and slapped the other side just as hard. In the dim light, he could see the red handprint he'd left.

He heard Leslie whine a little, and he knew it was affecting him. "I like playing, but I can't wait any longer, your ass is too much for me."

Aaron slid forward, nudging at him for a second before he gripped his hips and slammed into him all the way. He heard him let out a gasping moan and smiled. No one was going to hear them out here, and he was sure he could get him pretty loud if he tried. He leaned over him and reached down to stroke him a little to find him dripping profusely. That was a good sign, he thought.

"What a little slut you are, getting fucked outside at night, moaning like a bitch," he murmured into his ear before biting at it.

Again, Leslie let out a long drawn-out moan, and Aaron smiled as he continued to pound into him from behind. He could already feel him tightening up on him, and he knew that he wasn't going to last a whole lot longer. He pulled his face to the side and locked him into a kiss, reaching as much as he could into his mouth from the angle.

After a few minutes of torturing him with hard thrusts and light strokes, he was moaning and whining pretty steadily.

"Please, I need to..." he gasped out.

"Ya gonna come?" Aaron asked. "Don't you dare come until I tell you to."

He whimpered so nicely, and Aaron pulled all the way out before slamming forward again, getting a squeaking sound out of him. He leaned over again, this time grabbing him tightly at the base, causing him to squeeze down on him harder.

"Please, please, I need..." he huffed.

"What do you need?" Aaron asked. "Tell me."

"I need to come!" he begged. Again, Aaron thought how sweet that sound was. He smiled, releasing his cock and starting to stroke him as he thrust into him.

"What are you?" he asked as he sped up a little more.

"I'm your slut!" he answered immediately, and Aaron knew he must be really close to answer so fast.

"Good, then come, slut," he said as he flicked his hand faster over him.

A second more, and he felt him orgasm hard, tightening up on him until it was hard to move much. He thrust through it, pounding into him harder a few more times before he came himself. He leaned up and grabbed his hips as he held him like that for a moment before he pulled out. Leslie collapsed onto the blanket as soon as he let go of him.

"I've got grass in my mouth," Leslie muttered and spit.

"Well, at least the bugs left us alone," Aaron told him as he grabbed him up in a tight embrace.

"Now, I'm cold," Leslie said, and Aaron could feel the shivers going through his body now.

He grabbed his shorts and pants and helped him get into them before he got too much colder. Then they both laid down on the other side of the blanket on their backs. Leslie snuggled up onto Aaron's arm and stared at the sky.

"The stars are beautiful," he whispered finally.

"I think you're beautiful," Aaron told him.

He heard Leslie swallow noisily. "Even though I'm fucked up like this," he said softly.

"You're not fucked up," he assured. "You just have a problem you need help with. That's all."

"I thought I could handle it alone. But I was wrong. I'm too weak," he said and Aaron thought he sounded on the verge of tears.

"You're not weak," he said as he squeezed him closer to him. "Don't think that way. You've done your best."

"But I did this to myself. Why can't I fix it myself?" he asked.

Aaron didn't know how to answer that. "Look, you're strong enough to have made it this far. Now, you just have to be strong enough to ask for the help you need."

Leslie was quiet for a while as they both stared up into the night sky. It was a comfortable silence, though. There was no need to say anything because they both knew that the path ahead was still going to be rocky.

But they would take that path together.

# STRAY CAT CHRONICLES
## PART SIX

# Stray Thunder

Leslie sat in the waiting room beside Aaron uncomfortably. He had done everything to avoid this, but things had not gone the way he wanted them to go. Aaron was holding him accountable, which he knew he needed. His father had even gotten involved in the last couple weeks, which had led to a fight between him and his father. That fight had spawned another argument between him and Aaron, one that he had completely lost because he could not fight any longer.

They were right. He needed help. He just couldn't do this on his own and it was time for him to admit it.

"I'm nervous," Leslie muttered, gripping Aaron's hand tightly in his own. He hadn't let go since they came into the room despite the looks they had gotten.

"I know," he responded, squeezing his hand a little tighter. "But this is for the best, you know."

"How can I do this, though? Talk to a stranger like this? I don't know what to say or what to do when I get in there," he said, sighing as he glanced around the nearly empty waiting room. There was another person, a younger woman and what appeared to be her mom, waiting that came in after Leslie and Aaron.

"You can do it. I know you can," Aaron assured him, moving to put his arm around his shoulder and pulling him in tightly.

"Leslie Kirby?" a nurse said from the door.

"Um, yeah," he said, standing up shakily and looking at Aaron. "I'll be back soon. Don't leave."

"Wouldn't dream of it," Aaron told him as he went toward the nurse. Aaron knew what a big step this was for Leslie.

"This way, first we're going to take your vitals, and then Dr. Cossick will see you," the nurse, a redhead with a highly freckled face, told him.

They went to what looked like an office with a computer and a chair next to it. She had him get up on the scale and made a note of his weight. Then she put the oxygen reader on his finger and checked his blood pressure.

"Your blood pressure is a little high. Do you have problems with it normally?" she asked as she typed into the computer.

"Um, no, I think I'm just nervous," he said, shifting a bit uncomfortably.

"Understandable. Is this your first visit with a psychiatrist?" she asked.

He swallowed and nodded. "Yeah, I've never needed one before."

She smiled and nodded. "Dr. Cossick is a really great doctor. I'm sure you'll get along with him just fine."

After she'd finished, she took him to a smaller waiting room where he sat down. He wished Aaron was with him still. He folded his hands together and waited as patiently as he could.

"Leslie?" he heard and looked up to see a gentle looking man. He was in his thirties or forties, it was hard to tell for sure, and had neat brown hair. His eyes were a warm golden-brown color and looked sincere.

"Um, yeah," he said, standing up, keeping his hands folded together. "I'm Leslie."

Dr. Cossick smiled. "Come with me, and we'll sit and talk in my office."

Leslie followed him, looking around at the plain walls as he went. He hated doctor's offices because they were so sterile and this one wasn't much different. With his father being a doctor, he should have been used to them, but he still was put off by them. Dr. Cossick opened the door, though, and led him into an office that looked out of place compared to the other doctor's offices he'd been in. There was a large desk with a computer sitting to the side and a large, comfortable-looking couch sitting across from it. The room was warmly decorated with framed artwork of various types. Everything just went together and it felt...comfortable.

"Have a seat, Leslie, and we can start talking about what brings you here," he said and sat down in the large office chair at his desk.

Leslie sat down a bit nervously, afraid to get comfortable at first. "Um, well, I don't think it's such a big deal, but my b-boyfriend and my father think I need help, so I found you online and it said you worked with people with my problem," he told him, looking up at him.

"And what is your problem, Leslie?" he asked, watching him carefully.

Leslie cleared his throat, looking around the room a little. "Um, I have some issues with food and eating and stuff."

"Well, I work with a lot of people that have 'issues' with food and eating. I specialize in eating disorders. I use a treatment plan called Maudsley Anorexia Nervosa Treatment for Adults, called MANTRA. This treatment works well for people and would help you with your 'issues' as you call them." Dr Cossick said and smiled at him. "Do you want to get rid of these 'issues' you have with food and eating?"

"Well, yeah, I guess I need to," he said with a frown. "I mean, it isn't good, right?"

"Leslie, you're going to have to decide that you want to change things for anything I do to help you," the doctor explained, looking at him seriously.

Leslie shifted uncomfortably. "Well, I mean, Aaron, that's my boyfriend, he tried to help me eat normally, well, as he called normally. I just want to watch my calories and my weight. I don't think that's such a bad thing because I'm a swimmer and I need to stay in shape, you see."

"Are you making excuses not to change things, Leslie?" Dr. Cossick asked.

He looked up at the doctor for a second and didn't speak. "But if I don't keep an eye on what I eat, what if I gain weight again?"

Dr. Cossick glanced at the file on his desk where the intake paperwork was. "You talked about wanting to lose more weight. Is there a reason you think you need to lose more weight?"

"I'm a swimmer. Swimmers aren't supposed to be heavy or muscular, right?" he looked up questioningly.

"I think you're still coming up with reasons for your desire to control your weight," the doctor pointed out. "What exactly makes you want to control what you eat so much, Leslie?"

Before he thought about it, he blurted, "What else am I going to control?" Then his eyes widened, and he didn't know what to say.

"Do you feel out of control in your life, Leslie?"

He swallowed, chewing his lip for a second. "I guess, I mean, I think I feel like everything happens to me, around me," he said slowly. "Even getting together with my boyfriend. I feel like it just happened, and it wasn't my idea."

"Leslie," he asked, watching him. "Are you in a safe relationship?"

Leslie looked at him sharply. "Of course! I love Aaron!" He paused. "It's just that...well, it's like I've always just been along for the ride in my life. That things happen to me, and good or bad, I don't do anything to cause them to happen."

"Tell me, Leslie, how did you and Aaron get together?" he asked.

Leslie flushed immediately, looking away from him. "Well, it was just this one day, we got into a fight during swim class, and went back to the locker room, and I kinda told him that I was attracted to him, and um, things kinda went from there."

"But you were the one that told him you were attracted to him, weren't you?" Dr. Cossick asked calmly.

Leslie looked over at him and nodded. "Yeah, I guess I did."

"What would have happened if you hadn't told him that you were attracted to him?"

"Nothing," Leslie admitted. "I mean, if I hadn't said that he wouldn't have...and we wouldn't have...and we wouldn't be together now."

"So, you were in control of that situation," he pointed out.

Leslie stared at his hands for a minute and frowned deeply. "I...I never thought of it that way."

"What is it that you're really trying to do, Leslie?" he asked then.

"I don't know anymore," he responded quietly. "I thought I knew, but now I'm not so sure."

There was a long silence before the doctor spoke up again. "Let's talk nutrition."

"Nutrition?" Leslie asked.

"Yes," he answered. "What is healthy eating? What does that look like?"

"Ah, well, you've got to eat protein, carbohydrates, and fats every day in the right proportions, and take in enough calories to keep your body going. So, you have to keep a balance between what you input into your body and how much energy you expend." Leslie knew all these things, of course.

"You seem to know the basics of good nutrition." The doctor looked at him for a long time, and Leslie grew a bit uncomfortable under his gaze. "But you aren't adhering to the idea of good nutrition by limiting your calories too much."

Leslie licked his lips and thought about it. "But I have to keep track of the calories and not go over a certain amount."

"But is that certain amount enough to keep your body going, Leslie? Is it really?"

"Um, well, I think it's enough..." he trailed off.

Dr. Cossick leaned over and opened a drawer in his desk. He pulled out something that looked like a workbook. "I want to send you home with this. It's a cognitive behavioral therapy workbook just for anorexia."

Leslie took it and thumbed through it. He could do that, he thought. "So, I just work on this when I can?"

"Just when you're ready. Leslie, from your intake evaluation and what we've talked about here, I think you could be able to change things if you decide to. The question is, are you ready to make these changes?" Dr. Cossick asked him.

"I want to be okay, and I want Aaron and my family to stop worrying about me because I don't like that."

The doctor nodded. "Alright, tell me what you want out of our therapy sessions?" he inquired, tilting his head to the side and staring at Leslie.

"I want to get better," he said finally.

"That's what is necessary to get better," the doctor answered. "You have to have a desire to make these changes. I can help you, but it might take a while to get completely better. And you may always struggle with some of these things. You have to know that you have family and a boyfriend that are going to support you in this journey."

"Yeah," Leslie sighed. "I know, I just have to let them support me, right?"

Dr. Cossick smiled. "You do. Along this journey, you may uncover uncomfortable things about yourself, and that's okay. We'll work through them as they come up."

"Okay, I understand."

"We'll schedule you for ten sessions on a weekly basis, and then after that, there will be another ten sessions that might have some more time between them, depending on how things go with you. You can involve your family and your boyfriend in this process as much or a little as you want," he told him.

"So, Aaron can come with me to this?" he said, looking up.

"If you want him to come, you can allow him to do so," Dr. Cossick said with a small smile.

"Alright," he said and sighed.

Dr. Cossick stood up. "For today, I want you to look over the workbook and start filling out some of it. Share with Aaron if you're comfortable and talk about things as you work over them. Remember, it is up to you how much you involve him in your treatment."

Leslie stood and walked out of the office with him. "Thank you," he said, clutching the workbook to his chest.

Dr. Cossick talked to the nurse at the desk and told her to set him up for ten weekly appointments with him. They discussed a couple things and the doctor nodded, patting Leslie on the back and disappearing into the back again. He talked over the schedules with the nurse and got everything situated for him to come back the next week. He then walked out to the waiting room where Aaron was still waiting. He released a little sigh of relief. For some reason, he'd worried that he might have left or something. He had no reason to believe that he would, but he was feeling very insecure at the moment for lots of reasons.

Aaron looked up as he came out and stood up. "Everything go okay?"

"Yeah, it did. I like him," he said with a nod. "He gave me this," he showed Aaron the workbook. "So, I just have to start working on it."

"Good," Aaron said, putting a hand on his face. "You ready to go home?"

"Yeah," he said as he reached for Aaron's hand.

They headed out, ignoring the woman in the waiting room that glared at them as they left. Even Leslie managed not to be bothered by her this time. He had other things on his mind besides rude people who he had nothing to do with. As they got outside, he looked around.

"It's clouding up," he commented.

"Yeah, they said we might get thunderstorms tonight," Aaron commented as they headed to the car.

Leslie's step hesitated for a second. "Thunderstorms, huh?" he said with a frown.

Aaron glanced at him. "You okay?"

"Oh, yeah, fine," Leslie said as he walked around and opened the passenger door of Aaron's car.

"So, how'd the therapy appointment go?" Micah asked as they sat down at the café they were having dinner at with her and Aiden.

"It was good," Leslie said with a half-smile. "I like the doctor, so that's good. He gave me a workbook that I started filling in today," he said with a nod of his head.

"That's cool," Aiden said as the server brought over their drinks and sat them down.

Leslie stared at the menu, still calculating the calories as he looked it over. He had eaten twice today, small meals, but at least more than he had been eating. This was the first time in a while he'd tried going out to eat with anyone.

"Leslie, you decide what you want to try?" Aaron asked from beside him.

"I think so, but what if I can't eat it all?" he said nervously. He really didn't want to upset Aaron by not eating what he ordered.

"Then eat what you can," he said softly as the server turned toward them after taking Micah and Aiden's order.

Aaron ordered, and that left Leslie as the last one to put in his choices. "Um, here, this chicken salad," he said finally, thinking that it would be the most reasonable on calories.

No one said anything about it, though, for which he was glad. He really didn't want to have to try and stammer out a reason for what he was ordering. They talked about school and other things while they waited for their food. Leslie was still feeling a bit off when a loud crack of thunder caused the windows of the small place to rattle a little. He jerked, nearly knocking his drink off the table.

"You okay?" Aaron said, putting a hand on his back.

"Ah, yeah, thunder isn't my favorite thing," Leslie answered, heart racing a little. Great, of all the times to have anxiety about a storm.

Luckily, the rest of the dinner was uneventful. The storm seemed to be quieting down and Leslie had hopes that it was just going to pass them by. To Aaron's pleasure, he'd ended up eating over half of his salad. Leslie was glad that he had made Aaron happy because he was trying hard to do the things he knew he had to do so he could get better.

"Good night, guys," Micah said as they came out of the café.

Leslie gave her a hug quickly. "Good night. Be careful driving home."

"Yeah, looks like that storm isn't going to miss us after all," Aaron pointed out, looking up.

Just then, there was a rolling peal of thunder and a flash of lightning nearby. Leslie jumped a little and grabbed Aaron's hand. He felt Aaron squeeze his hand and he was glad for that. They watched Aiden and Micah pull out and leave the parking lot.

"You okay?" Aaron asked as they walked toward his car.

"Yeah, um, I don't really like storms like this," he admitted as he got into the passenger side.

"You never mentioned that before?" Aaron said as he started the car.

Leslie laughed a little nervously. "I think my anxiety is a little worse today. Sometimes it doesn't bother me as much, but today it seems to be."

"Ah, that's okay, Leslie-babe," Aaron said as they pulled out and headed to their apartment.

Before long, the rain started, and the lightning began to flash followed closely by cracks of thunder. Leslie felt his heart racing a little and thoughts began to impinge on him. They pulled up and got out, trying to avoid getting too wet as they took the stairs up to their place. They weren't entirely successful, and both started to strip off their wet clothes as they got inside.

A particularly loud crack of thunder made Leslie nearly jump out of his skin and yelp rather loudly. He felt Aaron's arms around his damp body, and he turned into him and buried his face into his chest. He hadn't had an attack of anxiety like this in a long time, and he had to wonder if it wasn't visiting the therapist that had triggered it.

"Leslie-babe, come on, let's go to bed," Aaron said softly, stroking his back gently.

"O-okay," he said, jerking and whining as another loud roll of thunder sounded.

After a few minutes, they'd both gotten into the bed, wet clothes piled on the floor.

Aaron was silent, still just holding him. The thunder was fading, though, the storm apparently moving quickly away. It had come on quickly, too, just like Leslie's anxiety. Leslie nuzzled up into Aaron's neck, tightening his grip around him.

"Yeah," he whispered. "I think I'm tired," he said softly, eyes fluttering against Aaron's skin.

"Let's sleep, babe," Aaron told him and hugged him close.

Leslie woke first the next morning as the light streamed in through the window curtains. He rubbed his eyes. He sat up and got up and went to the bathroom, looking at his face as he washed it with cold water. He'd told the therapist that he loved

Aaron. He realized how true those words were. He dried his face and went back to the bed, trying not to wake him.

He settled back into his arms and wondered at what the therapist had said about being in control of things. Was that what everything was about after all? He swallowed, pressing his head into Aaron's shoulder. He had Aaron now and he had good reason to get better, and his family and friends were going to support him in getting better, he knew. But at the bottom of it all, he had to wonder why he ended up like this?

He had decided to tell Aaron that he liked him. He knew Aaron now, and he knew that nothing would have ever happened if he hadn't done that. He had done that, no one else. He made the choice. He had to stop thinking like he hadn't, he realized. But there were so many things he hadn't been able to control in his life.

Like his mom's impending death.

He sighed, drifting between sleep and wakefulness for a while until he felt fingers threading through his hair again.

"Mornin'," he mumbled, turning his face up to lock eyes with the blue ones over him.

"How are you this morning?" Aaron asked, voice a little rough from sleep.

Leslie smiled, "I think I'm okay. It's kinda embarrassing, being afraid of a silly storm."

"Aw, babe, don't talk like that," Aaron said, pulling Leslie's head toward him and kissing his temple. "Nothing to be embarrassed about."

They were quiet for a few minutes until Leslie felt Aaron slide his hand down between his legs and press into him. "Now, what's this?"

Leslie flushed immediately. He squirmed to get away from his hand, but Aaron's other arm was locked around him. "Just morning stuff!" he tried.

"Nah, you've been awake for a while, haven't you?" he asked.

"Th-that's not true!" he gasped as he felt Aaron's hand grip him tightly. He could already feel Aaron's growing interest against his leg where it was lying on him.

"You never get this way in the morning," Aaron pointed out, starting to stroke him until he was whimpering quietly. "What should we do about it?"

"I don't know!" Leslie grumbled, looking away but feeling himself start to drip a little over Aaron's firm hand.

Aaron chuckled, moving to pull Leslie over on top of him and kissing his neck gently. "I can think of only one way to take care of my little slutty boy," he murmured, biting gently at the juncture of his neck and shoulder. "Since you started this, you can show me how good you are at riding my cock."

"But I didn't start it!" Leslie whined, gasping as Aaron shifted under him until his cock was pressing at his entrance, just slightly.

Leslie moved until he was straddling his thighs. He moved up until they were pressing against each other and bucked his hips against him. Aaron reached out and stroked them together and grinned at him. Leslie had no idea what was on his mind, but he was more than willing to have a morning romp as hard as he was right then.

"Yer beautiful, you know?" Aaron said, reaching out and brushing a hand against his jaw. "More beautiful than anyone in the world to me."

He felt his face heat and he ducked his head a little, leaning down to kiss Aaron's chest, tonguing his nipples gently as his hands squeezed his ass.

"You want to use that lube or you want to go without?" Aaron asked, fingers kneading the flesh under his hands.

"I like that lube, it feels good," he said, leaning over to open the bedside drawer and fishing out the bottle.

"Hmm, I do too," Aaron told him as he shifted underneath him until he'd slipped him up higher on him.

Leslie started to open the bottle to get some out, but Aaron suddenly shifted his hand underneath him and slipped a couple fingers into him roughly. He whimpered, putting his head down on his shoulder for a second. It kind of burned, the dry entry, but it still felt really good to his overheated body. He let him finger him for a while before he moved again, sliding down once more to straddle his thighs.

He opened the bottle and squeezed out enough on his hand, the mint smell filling the room immediately. He was still amazed at how strong the scent of the stuff was. It took no time at all to be everywhere. He liked it, though, because it kind of tingled too. He tossed the bottle onto the bed, and coated Aaron with it slowly, looking up at him the entire time. Aaron's eyes didn't move from his, and he could feel the heat from his gaze.

"You sure that's enough prep, babe?" Aaron asked, brow crinkling as Leslie moved up higher and pulled himself over Aaron while he steadied him with his hand.

"Uh huh. Sometimes, I like it that way," he said, feeling a blush start to form as he said it. Why did everything have to be so embarrassing?

He moved and slipped down on him, face scrunching a bit at the slight pain it caused him. He wasn't lying, there were times he craved the pain the connection between them brought him. It was somewhat grounding, to be honest. He slid down until he was sitting flat on his lap, breath coming in little pants as he got used to it.

"Okay, there?" Aaron said, hands stroking his hips as he looked at him with a concerned face.

"Yeah, feels good, just gotta get adjusted to it," he said a little breathily. "It's been a while since we've done it since we've been so busy."

"Hmm, yeah, and I missed being inside you," Aaron said, squeezing his ass tightly as Leslie started to move on him. "I think it's my favorite place to be."

"Sh-shut up!" Leslie said, using his legs to move up on him before dropping down hard.

Aaron grunted and arched back a bit. "Feisty," he muttered. "I like it."

Leslie spent the next few minutes working himself on Aaron until he found his prostate and gasped out, tightening up on him significantly. Aaron chuckled, thrusting upward hard, knowing that he'd hit his sweet spot then. The angle was about right, but Aaron had to help out because he could feel that Leslie's strength in his legs was waning after a while.

"Can you keep it up, or should we switch?" he asked, rubbing his back as he leaned over to kiss him.

"I'm fine!" Leslie snapped, renewing his efforts to move fast enough. "I can make you come like this."

"Oh, you can?" Aaron asked, biting lightly at his lips. "You've never been able to do it before."

"Well, I can do it!" he responded, frowning.

He slowed his hips and found Aaron's mouth, occupying himself for a time with a long, deep kiss until he had to breathe again. It gave his legs a minute to rest in that position. He could feel himself throbbing between them and he wanted to tell him to touch him, but he was still too embarrassed to do it. Aaron, though, knew what he wanted. He just wanted him to say it. Leslie leaned back, moving his feet to push up from the bed as Aaron met him. Finally, embarrassed or not, he couldn't take it.

"Touch me!" he gasped out, leaning back and bracing himself on Aaron's legs behind him.

"Where?" Aaron asked, smirking as he ran his hands up his stomach to pinch at his nipples.

"You know where!"

"No, I don't," Aaron told him. "You could mean anywhere."

Leslie had flushed red again and growled. "My cock, dammit!"

Aaron moved his hand down and began stroking him as he moved on him. "I know I can make you come like this. You might be able to make me come if you try hard."

"I am trying hard!" he sputtered, dropping down hard enough that it nearly hurt. "I want to come together!"

Aaron arched a brow at that because that was something they hadn't done before. "Ah, babe, just keep doing what you're doing, and you'll get me there. You're such a good slut for me, aren't you?"

"I am!" Leslie said as he moved again. "I'll make you come, I will!"

Leslie knew if he could just get Aaron close enough to the edge, when he orgasmed, he'd go too. They'd gone close to each other before, but never quite together. Aaron was doing what he could and before long, his nails were digging into Leslie's hips, so Leslie knew that he was getting close. He was holding on tightly because he was about to go himself, but he swore he wasn't going to go until he was sure that Aaron was going to come, too.

"I'm close, babe," Aaron growled, sliding his hand over and gripping him tightly as he rode him.

"Me too," Leslie gasped out finally after a second. "Just a little more..."

It hit him, then, hard. He'd been holding off as much as he could, and he felt it crash into him. Almost as soon as he did, he felt Aaron stiffen under him and quiver inside him. To be honest, it felt amazing from both sides to him, and he thought he was going to come unglued before he was done. He then fell to the side to avoid the mess he'd left on Aaron's stomach. Aaron leaned over, grabbing tissues from the box on the bedside table and cleaning himself off before he tossed them in the small trash can.

"Well, that was intense," Aaron said, turning over and sliding his arms around Leslie and engaging him in a long, languid kiss once more.

Leslie was still a bit out of breath. "Yeah, but I did it, dammit," he muttered.

"Yeah," Aaron said, brushing a hand over his head. "You did, didn't you? Such a good slut for me."

Again, Leslie felt his face heat up and he buried it in Aaron's chest. He nodded though. "Uh huh," he whispered.

They laid there until Aaron's alarm began to sound on his phone. He reached over and turned it off, nuzzling into Leslie's neck quickly as he rolled back over.

"Time to get up," he said. "Wanna take a shower together?" he asked.

"Yeah," Leslie said, sitting up slowly.

They got ready for their day as they always did. Spending perhaps a little extra time in the shower with each other than they normally did. They were on time, though, and had enough time to heat up the breakfast sandwiches they kept in the freezer for the mornings. Leslie dutifully ate his, though in his mind he kept track of the number of calories still.

"Oh, my workbook!" he said as they headed to the door. He turned back and grabbed it and clutched it to his chest. "I don't want to forget it on my first day using it!" he said.

Aaron kissed him on the head, and Leslie was proud of himself. Perhaps things were going to get better now. Perhaps getting help was the right decision.

# DEMONIC DESIRE

There was a simple village that was plagued by a demonic creature. To appease the creature, the village would send a maiden to the cave it lived in. The maidens would never come back, and the village, being a small one, began to run out of young women to send to the monster. No one knew who had decided that once a year on the summer solstice, a young woman was to be sacrificed to the monster. They just knew that each year, they had to take a sacrifice to the demon or else some unspeakable evil would befall the village.

When his sister Charity was chosen, Rain knew he had to do something. He would not let his sister be sacrificed to this terrible monster. He steeled his courage and determined that he would follow the procession up the mountain and kill the monster before it devoured his sister.

The morning the sun rose and there was a tearful goodbye between his sisters Amber and Charity. His father wept and Rain tried not to be afraid for her. Charity had been strong, though, and bid everyone farewell. Rain let them leave and then went to the house and retrieved the sword his father used to wield in a past war torn period. He knew how to use it basically, but he was not well trained. He climbed the side of the mountain, trailing the group that was escorting his sister.

He followed them closely and watched as his sister was tied to the stake at the top of the mountain pass. He waited until they had gone, leaving her there alone. He crept from the hiding place he'd been in and went to his sister.

"Rain!" she gasped as she saw him. "What are you doing here?"

"I'm saving you. You run back to the village. I'm going to go kill this demon. Then we don't have to fear it any longer," Rain told her. "I won't watch you be devoured if I can stop it. I can see the creature's cave nearby and will go there and destroy it."

"But Rain!" she gasped as Rain cut her free from the stake. "What do I tell them?"

"Tell them I went to kill the demon, and might not return," he said solemnly. "Go back with Amber and our father."

Charity, frightened beyond words, ran back down the path. Rain turned and walked up to the cave. It was dark and ominous looking, and he felt his heart beating in his ears. He held the sword and stepped forward into the darkness. His breathing was overly loud to his ears and he thought for sure this day would be his last. At least he had saved his sister, though. He just had to hope they wouldn't send her back after she returned to the village.

"Who disturbs my rest..." came a voice from the depths of the cave.

Rain swallowed the fear and moved forward, seeing some light ahead of him. He made his way to an open chamber in the cave with luminescent moss lining the walls. It gave enough light that he could see the underground lake that stretched out into the mountain. The sound of his breath was the only sound in the place. It was so quiet, the very walls seemed to swallow sound.

He felt like he was being watched.

"Little human, ya court yer death..." he heard and turned around, looking for the source of the voice. The voice came from all around him at once.

"I came here to fight for the life of my sister," he said, gripping the sword tightly in his sweaty palms. "I will see the end of the sacrifices!"

"Yer bold. Ya would stand against me?" the voice began to laugh and from the water, something pearlized gray began to emerge. It looked like a snake, but it was the size of a person as it slithered out of the water and reared up, towering over Rain and coiling its massive tail around and surrounding Rain in the center of its body.

Rain gasped, unable to run now, but he had no intention of running away. He could not. He held the sword up as the coil came closer to him. It was going to crush him to death, he knew, or it would try. He stabbed the sword into the flesh of the creature as it came closer to him. The blade cut through the skin, but instead of bleeding, a red foam emerged and healed it immediately. Rain's breath kicked up a notch and he tried again, but the foam kept coming out of the demon and it looked as though it had never been cut.

"Die!" Rain cried out as the coil reached him and began to squeeze him until he couldn't hold the sword any longer. He heard it clatter to the ground as his breath was squeezed from him. He knew it would be the end of him. He had accepted his death when the squeezing stopped.

"It has been a long time since a human has stood up to me." The pressure eased until Rain could take gasping breaths. "It makes me want to keep ya..."

Rain panted as the coil began to release and he watched as the snake became smaller then coalesced into a human form. It was similar to Rain's form, only with gray skin. Strange blood red eyes with orange irises stared back at him.

"Ya wish to end the sacrifices?" it said, a grin spreading across the face. "Give yerself to me willingly and they will end forever."

"Myself?" Rain took a gasping breath as it, he, came toward him closer and closer.

"I'm lonely. All alone, what's a demon to do?" he purred, putting a hand against Rain's face. "And I need someone that will stand up to me. I hate the mewling females they send me, but no one has ever asked for my preferences over the years."

Breathing quickly, Rain tried to think of any way out of this. He could still run, but somehow, he knew that this demon would catch him. His pearly flesh showed with the light that reflected off him. He had to be careful, he was going to stop the sacrifices one way or another. He swallowed against bile that tried to rise in his throat. There was a strange scent in the room, and he was getting dizzy. He started to say something, but he felt the world slide away from him as he collapsed into a heap on the floor.

When he opened his eyes, he was staring at the ceiling. For a moment, he wondered if everything had just been a dream, but then he felt something slide against the naked skin of his thigh and he gasped.

"Are ya awake?" he heard from near his ear.

Blinking rapidly, he turned his head to face the demon. He was nude, completely devoid of clothes, and laying in a pile of incredibly warm and comfortable furs. He glanced around, seeing nothing in the light of the luminescent moss except the demon who had him captive and an empty cavern.

"What did you do?" Rain asked, pushing himself to sit up amid the softness.

"Ya needed to relax," the demon said, nearly purring in his higher pitched voice.

"Y-you will stop the sacrifices? You really will?" Rain stammered, covering himself and crossing his legs as the demon looked him over.

"I promise. Become mine, forever, and they'll stop. I'll be satisfied, and have no need of sacrifices anymore," he said, moving closer until one long-fingered and black-nailed hand slipped over Rain's knee. "And my name is unpronounceable by humans, but you can call me Xeres. What is yers?"

"R-Rain."

"Rain," he repeated, sliding his hand up Rain's thigh slowly. "Would ya give yerself up for the benefit of the others? Or will ya run away from me? I won't stop ya if you leave. Yer clothes are over there."

Rain looked over and saw a pile of what appeared to be his clothes. His breath quickened in his chest. It was quite obvious what this demon Xeres wanted from him. But to end the sacrifices? Could he become this demon's toy? Could he endure whatever he wished to do to him no matter how humiliating and degrading it might be? Despite an initial horror at the thought, there was a part of him that was curious and wanted to find out exactly what this demon intended to do with him, no matter how depraved it might be.

"Ya haven't run away yet," Xeres said, slipping his hand over Rain's where he covered himself. "Do ya desire to know what I want?" he whispered, leaning in closer and breathing heavily against Rain's neck. "I'll tell you. I want to have yer body in every way I can. I want to fuck ya until ya scream in ecstasy because ya will feel good, amazing even. I'll make everything feel better than anything you can ever imagine."

Rain's body trembled under the near touches and the hot breath against his skin. The only contact between them was where Xeres's hand covered his own. He wanted more and he wondered if there was something wrong with him because of it. He should have been frightened out of his mind. This was a demon. This was the demon that had plagued his home village for many long years. Yet, here he was, about to lay down for him without much resistance at all. He wanted it to be only to end the sacrifices, but that wasn't it.

For the first time in his life, he wanted something for himself. He wanted to just feel and not have to worry about anything for a little while. He wanted to just be.

"Yer thinking it over," Xeres breathed out on his neck. "And I can feel ya struggling to hold yerself back. Come on, just let me have you."

"C-can't you just take what you want and be done with it?" Rain stammered, truly trying to keep himself from showing his desires.

Xeres leaned back, and Rain realized his body was slick like polished stone. It looked like a plain human with hair like Rain's, but he would have to appear in some way to Rain so they could interact. Who knew what his original form was, and what was simply an image to satisfy the onlooker?

"I'm a demon that makes bargains. The only reason I'm here is because a long time ago, someone in that little village down there made a bargain with me. However, instead of following through on their end of the bargain, they ran from the village, leaving me bound to this place until the bargain is fulfilled. That bargain was to send me a bride, willingly. The man and his daughter escaped the village the night before she was to be mine. So, ever since then, I've been bound to this mountain, and to that village, waiting for a bride to willingly come to my side to fulfill the bargain." Xeres smiled wickedly. "So, I'm asking ya to be my bride."

"But I'm not a woman!" Rain growled out, pushing Xeres's hand away from him, anger quelling the desire that was building in his gut.

Xeres giggled and pounced, suddenly pinning Rain to the floor with his mouth inches from him, and one pale leg lodged between Rain's, pressing into him hotly. "Stupid human, I'm a demon. Yer concepts of gender don't matter to me. I have no gender as you conceive it. I'm formless matter with conscious-ness. I am whatever I want to be. But I know how to pleasure." He grinned wider, tongue licking out and gently swiping at Rain's lips. "Let me show ya."

There was no hiding Rain's interest now as Xeres's body radiated heat that he could feel. Formless matter he may have been, but the body he was in now was so warm it was almost uncomfortably hot. Rain panted, staring into those strange colored eyes. Thoughts marched through his brain at rapid pace, and he knew that he'd never felt like this before.

"What is it, Rain?" Xeres breathed against his lips.

Rain felt his body throbbing in anticipation because somehow, Xeres was laying over him but holding himself up so that he was hovering an inch above his naked skin. He was so close to touching him but not quite.

"Alright. I'll be your bride. B-but you have to stop the sacrifices!" Rain found his hands insistently reaching around Xeres's back, touching the nearly hot flesh finally.

All at once, Xeres's body relaxed against him, and Rain gasped at the feeling of his skin touching him fully.

"Hmm, what shall I do first?" Xeres said, but it was quite obvious he was talking to himself, and not Rain at all.

Xeres moved down his body, almost slithering snake-like. His mouth hovered for a second over Rain's straining member, then he leaned down and swallowed him entirely. Rain's hands went for the messy dark head of hair as he moaned out loud. He could feel his throat constricting on him, and he wondered if this demon had to breathe or not. It was beginning to feel like he didn't.

"Oh, oh, no good, I'm going to... I'm going to... Oh!" Rain gasped out as he felt the orgasm slam into him.

Xeres suckled him until he was completely spent. Then he released him and pushed himself up on his arms. "Well, that was well-received."

Rain stared at him. Then, he yelped as he was picked up easily and flipped to his stomach. The furs were so plentiful, it didn't hurt at all. Then he cried out as he felt Xeres's fingers sliding against his entrance.

"What are you doing?" he asked frantically.

"Oh, getting to the good part," Xeres said, and Rain's eyes widened as he felt something slide into him.

Part of him wanted to tell him to stop. The oral pleasuring had been one thing, but this was another. Still, he didn't say anything because he was curious about what he was going to do, and it did feel good.

"Yer tight here," Xeres said, pressing what Rain assumed was his finger deeper into him.

"Why wouldn't I be?" Rain growled, but he couldn't help that his cock was twitching. "It's not like I've done this before!"

Again, Xeres gave that high pitched giggle. "Shh, ya need to just let me do what I want, and you'll feel so good ya won't know what to do with yerself."

Xeres pulled his finger back, then when he pushed it back in, it was slick with something warm, and Rain felt him slide a second finger in with the first. He couldn't help the moan that escaped his lips.

"W-what is that?" he whispered harshly.

"A secretion I can create," Xeres said. "It'll make this go a lot smoother."

Rain felt him move his fingers back and forth, going a little faster. He hummed to himself as he did it, as though he were really interested in what he was doing.

"I thought I could go slow and easy, but I can't," Xeres said, pulling his fingers out of Rain.

Rain turned his head and looked behind him. Xeres grinned broadly and got up on his knees, stroking himself. Rain's eyes widened and he stammered something about waiting a minute, but it went unheard as Xeres leaned forward and sheathed himself completely inside Rain. Rain gasped, the sensation of being filled so fully new and unusual. Surprisingly, it didn't hurt, he just felt the stretch and a little bit of burning sensation that quickly faded as Xeres thrust deeper and stroked something that felt really good.

Rain put his head down, but then felt something sliding around his thighs. He then jolted as something wrapped around his chest and lifted him up until he was sitting up on Xeres's lap.

He looked down to see dark tentacles wrapping around his legs and chest. He supposed he was a shape-shifting demon, after all.

"Oh, that's better," Xeres said, leaning over and sucking on Rain's neck. "Better position to put my dick in ya as deep as I can. Of course, if it isn't deep enough, I can make it bigger. What do you think?"

Rain shook his head. "It's big enough!" he said but even as he said it, he felt Xeres's cock thickening and lengthening inside him.

He looked down to see a bulge in his stomach as the tentacles writhed around him. Then, one wrapped around his cock and slid up and down. He panted, unsure if he could take all the stimulation for much longer. Xeres slipped his hands around and the tentacle around his cock began to tighten at the base of it, making it impossible for him to release. He groaned as Xeres's hands spread his legs wider and he felt the tentacles tighten around his thighs.

"Look at ya. Filled to the brim with cock and moaning like a bitch in heat. I like it, let's fill you up even more, what do you say?" Xeres giggled.

Rain didn't know what he meant, but he felt one of the tentacles slither around his cock again. He looked down and watched as it split, a tiny tendril separating from the larger tentacle. He frowned a second, wondering what it was going to do, then it began to work its way down inside his cock.

"What?" he gasped.

"Give it a minute," Xeres breathed on his neck as he licked his ear. "Just a little more."

Rain wasn't sure what he thought of this as the tendril worked further into him. Then it pulled back a little and began thrusting gently back and forth. He groaned, unable to come but needing to badly. Xeres began to thrust into him, his cock slipping easily in and out of him with whatever secretion he made. It rubbed against the spot inside that felt so amazing. He threwhis head back and made constant sounds, unable to hold them back now.

"Oh, yer insides are mine, I'll paint them white with my come. I'll mark you as mine, inside and out, and no one will ever come between us. Yer gonna be mine from now on, and I'll do this as many times as I want, and you'll enjoy every minute of it," Xeres growled as his thrusts began to speed up.

"Oh, please, let me come!" Rain groaned.

"You want to come?" Xeres whispered, slowing down to a stop suddenly.

Rain panted. "W-what...don't stop..."

"Oh, yer gonna come, aren't you, when I tell you, and not a second before," Xeres said, licking languidly as Rain's neck as he slowly began thrusting into him again. "When I mark you, there's no turning back," he said, his voice taking a more serious tone.

"Mark me!" Rain gasped out. "Make me yours forever!"

Xeres giggled again, the high-pitched sound reverberating off the cavern walls. His thrusts began to pick up speed and the plunging tendril began to work in Rain's cock again. Rain felt his sweet spot stimulated again from the inside, and glancing down, saw the bulge in his stomach as Xeres's cock filled him completely. He was going to wait until he was told to come, though, like Xeres said.

The tendril slipped out, and the tentacle that was tightened around the base of his cock began to release. It took all of Rain's self-control not to come right then as it began to loosen. He panted and moaned with each thrust into him, his body as hot as Xeres's right then.

Xeres leaned forward, kissing his shoulder gently, then whispering, "Come."

Rain felt it slam into him at that one word, and as soon as it did, Xeres bit down on his neck. Rain cried out in pleasure and pain, though he was finding the two morphed together in some strange combination that felt amazing to him. He'd never experienced such an intense orgasm in his life, and when he opened his eyes, he noticed red-tinged black mist coiling around them. He felt Xeres slide out and the tentacles slithered away, laying him down on the furs, somehow missing the wet mess under him. He felt Xeres's arms go around him, and the world faded from him for a little while.

"You managed to convince the demon to stop taking the sacrifices?" Rain's father said.

Rain stood before him, barefoot, wearing a white robe. "It's more involved than that, but basically, yes. It's a bargain. I agreed to be his bride, for want of a better word."

His father blinked in surprise. "His bride?"

Rain colored and looked away. "You see, a long time ago, a man struck a bargain with him, and that bargain was to give him a willing bride. Before he could present his daughter to him, the man left, running away with his daughter. That's why the sacrifices started, to try and appease him after he was enraged at the bargain not being fulfilled."

"So, you fulfilled the bargain," his sister, Amber, said. Charity stood beside her already crying.

Rain nodded. He pulled down the side of the robe, revealing the fresh wound on his neck. "Doing so binds me to him forever, so I won't die. I'll be with him as long as he lives, and he's immortal."

His father sighed. "Will you stay close?"

"With the bargain fulfilled, he can leave the mountain now. But because of you and the girls, he's agreed that we can stay on the mountain until you pass from this world." Rain smiled a little sadly. "It will be hard, though, to watch you grow old while I remain frozen in time."

"You're okay with this?" Charity said tearfully. "It's all because of me!"

Rain moved forward and hugged her to his chest. "Don't cry for me, Charity. I'll have a new life, but I won't leave you, I promise."

Several hours later, Rain made his way up the mountain with a basket of treasures his family wanted him to keep with him. He came to the cave and couldn't believe that days ago, he'd come here to kill Xeres. He went into the cave and was met by manic giggles.

"You've returned," he heard and around him, a black mist coalesced into Xeres's human form that was beginning to take a more defined shape the more he took the shape. His hair was now long and black, and his skin had taken on a tanner quality rather than the stone-like gray. "I knew you would come back, though."

"Of course," Rain said, moving into the cave toward the back where the furs were piled up.

"What did ya tell them?" Xeres asked, following him.

Rain slipped out of the robe and crawled back into the furs. "The truth. I'm a demon's bride and won't die. There were tears, but they were happy we weren't leaving."

Xeres's robe disappeared, and he piled into the furs with Rain, arms slipping around him from behind. "Good."

Rain couldn't help the smile that came unbidden to his lips. This was his life now, the companion to a demon for eternity. He supposed there were worse ways to spend it.

# His Fantasy Made Real

## A Chains of Fate Story

Elliot Turner thought he had an easy life. He was a student at the University of Missouri in St. Louis. He struggled a bit with his self-esteem, but it was nothing he couldn't overcome. He was overly self-conscious about his weight but tried not to let it bother him. He was also relatively short, only five feet five inches, which made his weight a problem for his height, leaving him with a rather chubby figure around the middle. He had tried working out in high school, but it had been hard to keep up with it once he started college. Besides, he was too busy with his coursework to handle it. So to compensate, he became a serial dater, always with different girls. None seemed to stick, though, and he rarely had a second or third date with the same girl.

Then one night, Andrew, his dorm roommate, was watching something on his phone. It sounded like porn, but he didn't hear a woman's voice.

"Dude, you gotta see this," Andrew muttered. "This is the sickest shit I've ever seen."

"Really?" Elliot was curious and went to Andrew's bed to look at his phone.

"It's three guys going at it with another dude. Can you believe it?" Andrew said in a disgusted tone. "It's bad enough it's all dudes, but the way they're doing it, they're raping the other guy! I mean, people actually enjoy shit like this?"

Elliot stared at the video in disbelief as a strange feeling washed over him. Not only was it gay porn, but it was also gang rape. Three men were forcing themselves on another man. Elliot's heart sped up, and his breath became rapid. His mouth went dry, and he had no idea what to do with his feelings. It was perverse. It was twisted. It was the most amazing thing he'd ever seen.

Afterward, he went back to his bed. The problem was that he kept seeing and hearing the video in his mind, no matter how hard he tried to forget it.

It weighed on his mind over the next few weeks. He had to have something wrong with him. He just had to. The way he was feeling couldn't be normal, he thought. Not for a straight guy who was just your average guy. Something had to be off in his brain, something sick and twisted. But they made the video for people who liked that kind of stuff, people who enjoyed watching something like that. People who wanted to participate in something like that. But that was the problem he had.

He didn't want to participate by perpetrating a gang rape like that. No, the problem was that he very much wanted to be gang-raped like that.

Now, he lay in bed under the covers with his earbuds and watched the tiny images dance on his phone. He was vaguely glad his roommate was on a date tonight and would sleep at his girlfriend's house. His breath was bated as he watched the setup for the video unfold. It was typical for this type of video; a young man goes to the wrong part of town at night. First, he meets a dark figure, then more appear. Elliot's heart beat faster, expecting what he guessed he was about to see.

He slipped his hand down to stroke himself, finding the arousal almost painful. The young man was grabbed, stripped of his clothes, and thrown to the ground as they laughed at him. Elliot could see he had genital piercings and vines tattooed across his side. One of the men, with ashen hair, came up with some rope, tied his arms behind his back, and then cinched his ankles to his thighs. Elliot's hand slipped up and down his dripping length as he started to pant a little. The first man pushed him forward and began to take him roughly from behind. Another one forced his mouth open and began to violently fuck his mouth. It was almost too much for Elliot to stop going over the edge immediately, but he slowed down because he didn't want to come until he was done watching the video.

He bit down on his lip hard because he was throbbing with need by this time, but the video wasn't entirely done yet. After the two guys were done, they flipped the bound one to his back on the ground, forcing his legs apart when the third guy came forward and pinned him harshly as he brutally ground into him. Now, Elliot grabbed himself tightly at the base to try and stop from coming. The video was good quality and was longer than the other gang rape videos, even on the small phone screen. The young man on the screen was crying as one of them pushed his head back and began to come onto his face.

The video ended abruptly, and Elliot wondered if there was more. He'd have to look and see if he couldn't find a more extended version of it. It must have been cut from a longer piece. He put his phone to the side and reached down with one hand while stroking himself. Again, he slipped two fingers into himself, hissing at the sudden stretch. This time he was too impatient to go slow. If he had his place, he would have ordered something bigger, but he couldn't have something like a dildo or a vibrator around in the dorms. That was asking for trouble.

As it was, he imagined himself in the place of the young man on the video, being held down, fucked mercilessly, used like a cock sleeve, and nothing more... It only took a few moments until he came all over his hand, quite a bit because it had been a while since his roommate had gone away for the night. He grabbed the tissues, cleaned himself up, tossed them in the trash, and straightened his pajamas. His heart was still beating too fast, and the images repeatedly replayed.

A couple of weeks later, he'd been looking for similar videos, and someone had posted a link in the comments on the video he'd found. The link was for a website called the Real Fantasies Forum. The comment said it was good for people who liked this kind of thing. Moreover, the person said the forum was based in St. Louis, and sometimes there were meetups in the city.

After registering for the website, he browsed around the place to find it was for people who liked the same things that he did. He excitedly read about other people's experiences, their fantasies, weird feelings when they saw violent imagery, all of it. He couldn't believe there were other people like him. He didn't feel as alone as before. He noted that there were both women and men on the forum. There were subforums for straight men, gay men, straight women, gay women, bisexual men, and bisexual women. He went to the forum for straight men and was disappointed; it was all women dominating men. Some talked about having a woman peg them with a strap-on, and while it sounded hot, it wasn't what he was looking for. He frowned and chose the forum for gay men and found just what he was looking for.

But he wasn't gay. At least he didn't think he was gay. However, he frowned when he found precisely what he sought in that subforum. Maybe he was gay? Now he had no idea what to think.

No, I'm not gay, he thought and closed the page. He wasn't. He was straight, and straight men didn't fantasize about being raped by other men. He swallowed hard and vowed not to return to it again.

Instead, he signed up for some dating apps and started dating some girls. It was nice, and he enjoyed himself. It even led to sex a few times. But it wasn't the same. He couldn't get off unless he started thinking about one of the videos he had seen. He didn't know what to do but knew he was confused. So, back to the Real Fantasies Forum, he went. He posted some questions about if it was normal for a straight guy to have those kinds of fantasies. He got a resounding no; straight guys wouldn't fantasize about other men doing them; it would be women.

Now he was even more confused than before. He'd never questioned his sexuality before; he'd never had a reason to. However, now, with the replies he was getting, he had to wonder. He thought about every date he'd ever had with a girl and how they never felt right. Something was always missing, and he had never been able to put his finger on it. And after he found the videos, he had to think of them while having sex with a girl. He knew it couldn't be normal. But he still liked girls a little bit. So maybe he was bisexual. Then again, did he really like girls, or did he try to like girls because that's what he was supposed to do?

Then he came across a thread. It talked about fulfilling fantasies and what people would do to fulfill theirs. People were discussing arranging meetings with strangers to act out the scenarios in their heads. They were talking about doing the very thing he wanted more than anything. What's more, some of them were in St. Louis. There were also posts from other cities around the US and even other countries, but other people were from St. Louis. Then there was a link posted by someone from the forum. It said it was for people in the area looking to get their fantasy fulfilled.

With bated breath, he opened the link and found himself on a website with a few questions. Name, address with entry codes, phone number, and fantasy were the only things asked. In the fantasy section, it said to include a safe word to stop a scene. He thought about it a while, then picked the word "pickles" because he wouldn't say pickles in the throes of sex. He checked the site address; it was still from the Real Fantasies Forums, just a different section. He hesitated. What would happen if he filled this out? Would someone come to him? Would some random stranger text him out of the blue? He swallowed, and before he knew it, his fingers were typing out the details of his deepest, darkest fantasies. He submitted it. A popup confirmed his submission and then returned him to the previous forums.

Now, he guessed he would have to wait.

After two months, nothing had happened, and Elliot got into a routine of living a relatively everyday life for a college student. He would still watch the videos on weekends when his roommate was gone and often read through Real Fantasies Forum, answer posts, and make new ones. They make excellent video recommendations, he found, and new websites he had never heard of with pictures and gifs. But, honestly, he had almost forgotten about signing up for the questionnaire. When he did think of it, he imagined no one read those, and it was just for them to collect information. Yet, strangely, he'd gotten no spam despite giving all of his personal information.

He was still going on dates through a dating app he liked. No matter what happened, they left him unfulfilled, and now that he had explored it, he knew why, but he didn't want to put himself in any real danger. He just wanted to feel like he was in real trouble.

He sighed, changing his clothes for his date tonight. His current roommate, James Reyes, lying in bed, looked up at him. "Well, well, another date Casanova? What's that, the third one this week?"

Elliot smirked. "Yeah, yeah, just can't seem to find the right girl," he mumbled with another sigh as he finished buttoning up his shirt. "But this girl is cute, look." He passed over his phone to show him a picture.

"Holy breasts Batman!" James exclaimed. "She's got cleavage for miles. But she's got pink hair. You know what they say about the ones with strangely colored hair."

"What do they say about them?" Elliot sat down to tie his shoes.

"Well, you know, something," James stammered, obviously not knowing more about the subject.

"Ha, well, see you in the morning if all goes well." Elliot smoothed a hand through his longish blond hair and put his phone in his pocket. He grabbed his keys before heading out the door.

"Don't do anything I wouldn't do! Hell, don't do anything I would do!" James called after him.

Elliot was meeting this girl at Randy's. It was a short drive. He thought it would be the perfect place for good food, which was relatively cheap. He immediately pulled up and saw her, so he parked beside her. She was leaning back on a blue sports car, smoking a cigarette. He didn't remember it saying she smoked on her profile. Well, one little thing wouldn't matter. He'd tolerate the smoke because she was gorgeous. She was all curves and wearing a black dress that accentuated everyone. She did have brightly dyed pink hair in a short cut around her face. The color accented her tan skin nicely. And, as his roommate had pointed out, she had large breasts. He walked up to her, waving as he approached.

"You must be Elliot. Nice to meet you. I'm Angelica. Let me put this out, and we can go in." She smiled.

Now that he was seeing her in person, he wondered exactly how old she was because she was older than twenty. There was no way she was less than twenty-five or so. He shrugged. He could handle an older woman. She was also taller than him, he noted, especially since she had on heels.

Once inside, the server seated them at a table and asked, "What'll ya have to drink?"

"Just a water for me," Elliot replied.

Angelica smiled, moving her rolled silverware to the other side of the table. "Iced tea, sweet," she told the server.

After the server left the menus, they looked over the food choices. "Do you come here often?" Angelica asked.

"Oh, just now and then," he answered, still deciding what to eat. He had brought his previous date to this same Randy's. He'd been worried about getting the same server, but he'd gotten lucky, and they had a different one.

"I haven't been out to eat in a while," Angelica said, putting down the menu and looking across the table at him. "But I know what I want already."

"Really? That was quick," he commented, deciding on his food just as the server returned.

"I'll have the chef's salad," Angelica told her.

"And I'll have a bacon cheeseburger and fries."

"All right, we'll have it right out for ya," the server said, leaving them alone.

Elliot smiled across the table. "So, tell me about yourself."

"Oh, I could talk about myself all night. I'm a photographer for local magazines like After Dark and St. Louis In Focus. I've worked as a freelancer for a long time now, ever since I graduated. I went to school at UMSL and saw on your profile that you go there too." She sipped the tea thoughtfully.

"Yeah, I'm in the nursing program," he said, nodding as he sipped his water.

"Nursing? I don't hear too many guys who go into the nursing field. What made you decide to go into that?"

"Well, I've always liked caring for other people. I thought about being a doctor, but you know, it's the nurses who spend the time with the patients, not the doctors."

"What type of nurse do you want to be?"

"Oh, I'm thinking about neurology or oncology. The only thing I'm not really interested in is delivering babies. I mean, I know I'll have to do an obstetrics rotation, but I'd rather not it be my particular field, you know?" he sighed, thinking about it.

"That's cool, though."

"I take it you went to school for photography?" he asked.

"Oh, yes, I love photography. I could spend hours talking about it, but I'm sure you're not interested in all that stuff."

"Well, I'm interested in what you're interested in," Elliot responded.

"Aw, that's sweet of you. Hmm, let's see. As I told you in my messages, I use my brother's car. His name is Dean. He works full-time but takes night classes out at UMSL too. He's got a roommate named David, who is also going to school. Let's see, oh, I hang out a lot with them and a friend of ours named Tommy. Tommy has his own place, though. We often have dinners together. I'm really close to my brother, well, I call him my brother, we're actually childhood friends, so we see each other a lot, and I see David with him all the time. We also have another friend a bit older than us named Robert, whom I've met a couple of times. We had dinner with him a few weeks ago, but it was nice because he paid for everyone," she told him, crossing her arms over her chest as she talked. "Dean was glad to let me borrow the car for tonight. He thinks it's funny when I have dates because eventually, whomever I date has to meet him. He's a tough guy, but only on the outside. He's really a teddy bear; you know the type."

"Oh, yeah, sure." Elliot nodded.

"David's a great guy too. He's been a really great friend to Dean over the last few years. They started in the same dorm room at UMSL, and things just went from there. Oh, I'm the older one, by the way, but he takes care of me even though I try to take care of him. We have a lot of fun as a group, you know?" she said, reaching up and smoothing a hand over her short, pink hair. "Tommy's got a girlfriend, but they're open about other people, so he has side chicks all the time, but at least they know they're on the side. Dean and David are both single right now, but they date people now and then."

Elliot didn't know what to think of all this talk of other guys, but he guessed she must have been really close to them.

They looked up to see the server coming over with their food.

"Oh wow, that was fast. They're really on the ball here tonight," Elliot commented as she sat the plates down. He was glad for the distraction because listening to her go on about her male friends was strange.

They ate in silence for a few minutes until she spoke up again. "So, you get lots of dates on the app?"

"Um, yeah," Elliot said before he thought better. "Haven't found the right one, though."

"Aw, that's cute. So you're looking for the girl you'll spend a lifetime with, huh?" She grinned.

"I guess you could say that. I don't fit any of the matches I've made so far. So why are you on a dating app?" Elliot asked. "I mean, you seem to have everything going for you; why in the world would you need to come to online dating?"

Angelica smiled broadly. "Oh, just a little diversion. Sometimes I like to go out and have a good time without stress on the dating scene. It can be nice to go out without expectations, you know." She shrugged.

Elliot frowned a little because he had some expectations, and they led back to her place for the night. He cleared his throat. "Do you have any other family? I mean, other than your friend, Dean?"

"Not really. That's why Dean and I got so close. I didn't have any brothers or sisters, and neither did he, so we just kinda watched out for each other like family. I had a pretty shitty father who left when I was nine, and Dean's dad was always amazing and helped my mom out with stuff when she needed it. His mom was real nice, too. She always made cookies when I came over. It's a wonder I wasn't obese as a child from how that woman cooked!" She laughed and took another bite.

Elliot shifted a little uncomfortably at the mention of weight. So far tonight, he hadn't been thinking about his own. He smoothed a hand over his stomach under the table and smiled despite the sick feeling it left in the pit of his belly.

"My mom wasn't much of a cook," he said. "We ate a lot of takeout when I was growing up. I grew up in St. Peters, and that's where I went to school. Are you from St. Louis or somewhere else?"

"St. Louis my whole life!" she exclaimed, picking up her glass and taking a long drink. "You didn't say if you had any brothers or sisters?"

"Oh, I actually have four. Three older sisters and a younger brother. We're all close together in age, though, so my oldest sister is only five years older than me." He smiled, taking a bit to think about how to explain the next part. "But my mom is raising one of my sister's kids right now."

"Oh really? How'd that happen?"

"Well, Daniella got into drugs when she was a teenager and ended up pregnant. She's twenty-three now, but she's still out there partying it up. So, my mom has custody of her son. He's a great kid, but he had some birth defects from her being on meth while she was pregnant." He paused, sighing. "Albert is his name. He has some intellectual delays and some behavior issues. But my mom's working on it with him, and he's not doing too bad. He's come a long way since he was born early and tiny, so that's good."

"I'm sorry to hear your sister isn't in a good place; it has to be tough on the whole family." She had a look on her face that Elliot wasn't sure how to place.

"Yeah, holiday dinners are always a trip," Elliot smiled wanly. Suddenly his burger didn't look as appetizing as it had.

"What about your other sisters and brother?"

"Oh, that's not too bad. My oldest sister, Candance, is married and has two kids already. She lives in St. Peters still. That's where my parents live; then there's Brandy. She's only a year older than me, so she's still in school. She's going to Lindenwood, however. She's in some program for sociology. But, then, I'm closest to my little brother, Jason. He is two years younger than me and just graduated high school. He started at UMSL this fall, undeclared major so far. He doesn't know what he wants to do yet." He grinned a bit. "Boys gotta stick together with all those older girls!"

"I imagine," she said, putting her fork on her mostly empty plate.

Elliot finished the burger, his appetite returning after they got off the subject of Daniella. "You said your dad left, is your mom still around?"

"Oh yeah, she's still around. I see her about once a week. So we keep up with each other pretty closely."

The server came and cleared their plates, leaving the ticket. Elliot picked it up and pulled out his card to pay. He always paid for his dates, which was why sometimes he had spaces of time he didn't date when he was low on funds.

"So, what do you want to do after this?"

"Well, dinner and a movie are always fun," she mused. "There's a couple of good ones showing tonight. Unless you want to see a play I've been dying to see."

"A play? Which one?"

"Much Ado About Nothing. I have a weakness for Shakespeare. It's a new theater company which just started up. Oh, but we probably won't be able to get tickets. So, I guess a movie is our only choice," she said a little sadly. "I'll have to catch the show before it ends."

Glad he'd saved up the last couple of weeks, he smiled at her. "Awesome. Let's go."

"Oh, why not just take my car?" she mentioned as they got up to pay.

"Uh, sure, I guess, but what about mine?" he asked as they approached the counter. He paid the ticket, signed the receipt, and added a suitable tip.

"Make sure it's locked up, and I can bring you back to it after we're done." She smiled at him as they headed out the door.

Elliot nodded. "All right, sounds good. No reason to waste gas, right?" He smiled again. "Let me make sure it's locked," he said, pulling out his key fob and clicking it again. "Okay. Shall we?"

"Please." She walked over to her borrowed car. It was a very nice car, Elliot thought as he got in. He wasn't a car guy, but he thought it seemed fancy. "It's my brother's like I said," she commented as she buckled her seatbelt.

"Oh, yeah. It's a nice car."

They headed out to the movie theater and readily agreed on a film to see. They got a couple of drinks and a tub of popcorn. Elliot was looking forward to this movie, but halfway through it, he realized he hadn't made any moves on her. And she didn't seem to be giving any signals either. He swallowed and wondered what she was thinking. For the rest of the movie, he thought more about it and missed the ending because he was so distracted. The way things were going, he would end up back at the dorms tonight.

"That was great!" she exclaimed as they returned to the car. "I had a wonderful time!" She smiled at him.

"Oh, me too!" Elliot agreed. "What now?"

She frowned and tapped her chin. "I know; we should go back to my place for a nightcap; what do you say?"

Elliot grinned. "Oh, sure, that sounds like fun." So maybe tonight wouldn't be a wash after all.

They arrived at a lovely house away from everything outside the city in Chesterfield. No neighbors were nearby, and a thick hedge surrounded it, and she gestured for him to follow her. He did so, watching how her skirt rode up her thigh a little as she walked. Finally, she led him in and to a kitchen, where she poured them each a glass of wine.

"Are you even old enough to drink?" she asked, smiling. "Your profile said you were twenty-one, but I don't believe it."

Blushing a little, he ducked his head. "Well, I'm twenty, so I'm close enough," he muttered, sipping his wine.

"Want a little tour?" She finished her wine in one long drink, surprising him.

"Uh, sure." He downed his glass to catch up with her. If he felt a little heady, he didn't let it bother him. He wasn't used to alcohol very often, after all.

She led him around, showing him all the rooms until they reached the last room: her bedroom.

"And this is my room," she said, gesturing to the closed door.

"Oh, um, can I see what it looks like?" he asked, trying to seem casual about it. This is where he had hoped to end up for the night.

Smiling again, she glanced between him and the door. "Oh, are you sure you want me to open this door?"

He arched a brow at her and nodded. "Um, yeah, that's what I said..."

"Okay," she smirked and pushed the door open, stepping back to let him in. The room was pitch black, however. Because the hall light only lit up the very inside of the doorway, he couldn't see anything beyond a couple of feet. "The light switch is just in the door there." She stepped back.

Elliot was a bit confused at how she was acting, but he stepped into the doorway and reached for the light.

Immediately, someone grabbed him by the wrist and yanked him into the dark room. He gasped as he felt another person grab his other arm. He still couldn't see anything, but now he heard breathing. There were people in this room, hiding in the dark!

"Hey, let me go!" he yelped, and then someone wrapped a piece of fabric between his lips, forcing his mouth open and gagging him.

"Mumph!" he tried as both arms twisted behind him, one on top of the other and rope against his skin. They were tying his arms behind his back! His heart rate skyrocketed, and he wondered what was happening here.

"Angelica, be a dear and hit the light," he heard a man's smooth voice from nearby.

Suddenly, the room was awash in light. It took a second for his eyes to adjust, but then he could see clearly. He was standing at the foot of a king-size sleigh bed in the center of the room. At the head of it sat a man with dirty blond hair pulled back in a ponytail and tattooed sleeves on both arms. Standing beside the bed was a man with long, dyed green hair and piercings in his eyebrows, nose, and ears. Both were grinning at him. The only other thing in the room was a chair in the corner where a man with short brown hair was sitting with his legs crossed. Someone was behind him, hands locked around his biceps. He heaved rapid breaths as he stared at the man in the chair.

"Ah, what have we here?" the brown-haired man said as he stood up slowly. His eyes were dark brown, and Elliot could see he was tanned. He was wearing a beige business suit and a red tie. He walked over and cupped Elliot's face in his hands, and when Elliot jerked away from him, he slapped him. "No, no, none of that. You don't seem to realize your position, do you?"

Elliot turned to look at the one holding his arms behind him. This man was much taller than Elliot, with darkly tanned skin, a shaved head, and a broad grin. Elliot swallowed, feeling spit drip from the edges of his mouth. The sound of a shutter caused him to growl against the gag, and he turned his head the other way to see Angelica standing just inside the door, fiddling with a camera.

"I told you I was a photographer, Elliot," she said as she moved closer. "I didn't tell you that while our date was fun, it wasn't going anywhere. I'm a lesbian and very happy with my girlfriend, Terri."

Elliot's eyes widened. Was it all a lie? The whole thing?

"He's fit enough," came the gruff voice from the guy holding him. "A little meaty, but he's all right." Elliot struggled again, but the guy had an iron grip on him.

Angelica snapped a picture, the flash blinding him for a second. "I believe I've already told you about everyone tonight. This is Robert," she said, gesturing to the brown-haired man before him. He turned forward to stare at him. "Behind you is Dean, my brother. And the one on the bed there is David, and the last is Tommy."

He tried to say, "What do you want with me?" but it came out, "wot oo oo ant ith ee," and the one holding him from behind jerked him a little.

"Oh, we're going to have some fun, Elliot, was it?" Robert murmured, touching his chest over his heart for a second. "But first, let's get rid of these clothes. They're in the way."

Elliot struggled again, but Dean only yanked on his arms more. Robert started unbuttoning Elliot's shirt very slowly. He looked down, watching him go down the buttons. He was panting behind the gag when the last one came undone, his shirt falling open. Robert smoothed his hands over Elliot's chest, pausing to pinch painfully at his nipples. He had never been touched like this by another man, and no one had ever messed with his nipples. It hurt, but at the same time, he liked the feeling of having them touched.

"Good, good, he's responsive. So it won't be a boring night after all." Robert smiled as his fingers went for the button on

Elliot's slacks. Elliot tried to move away from the wandering hands, only to have Dean smack the back of his head.

"Be still, dammit, or yer gonna get hurt worse," he growled, and Elliot didn't know what to do.

He felt his shirt pull down his arms, and Dean tied it around his bound forearms. Robert slipped his slacks down off his hips. He pulled on the band of his boxer shorts and slipped them down so both pooled at his feet. Robert hummed and reached between Elliot's legs, grasping his cock and stroking him. Elliot winced, the touching setting his body on fire as excited as he was. In the back of his mind, the word "pickles" flashed but was at once dismissed.

"Ah, look, I think he's enjoying himself," Robert said after a few moments of stimulating him.

"No, op!" he yelled through the gag.

"No one here will stop until you are well and truly fucked, do you understand?" Robert snarled as he grabbed his chin and tilted his head toward him. "Do you get what's happening now?"

Elliot couldn't help the sudden wave of intense arousal over him. He was scared out of his mind, but somehow it was exciting at the same time.

"Come on, Robert, I'm getting bored," David complained from the bed. "You can't just play with him all night. I wanna see some tears in those beautiful blue eyes of his."

Robert smirked. "Of course, I wouldn't want anyone to get bored. Dean lay him down over here on his stomach," he gestured toward the bed.

He fought the hold and stumbled as Dean dragged him towards the bed, but he couldn't escape as he bent over it. He felt someone removing his shoes, pants, and boxers from around his ankles. He turned his head to the side and glared at the one named David.

"He's got fire; I give him that." David grinned, reaching out to ruffle a hand through Elliot's hair.

"Ng!" he grunted, shaking his head.

"He's a little chunky, but he's got a nice, tight ass," he heard one of them say and felt hands sliding against his ass.

"But has he had it plowed before, is the question." Dean slid his hand down and shoved a finger deep inside him. It was somewhat painful but didn't seem as painful as he expected. He guessed they were using something slick to make it easier.

"Ah!" he gasped, feeling the strange sensation of someone else touching him there. It wasn't like when he did it himself; it felt immeasurably better.

"I think he plays with himself," Dean said, twisting and working another finger into him, making Elliot whine. "He's not as tight as he should be if he were really a virgin. Wonder if he's got toys."

Elliot squeezed his eyes shut and tried to think about anything but the questing fingers inside him. Elliot hummed loudly as he brushed up against something that felt different and good, something he'd never reached with his fingers. He felt him put a hand on his lower back to hold him in place and then start plunging his fingers harder into him. He felt tears already. He couldn't stop them, whether, from shame or frustration, he didn't know.

"Here, let me get a good angle," Angelica said, her voice making him open his eyes and look up. She had appeared where Elliot could see her. She snapped a picture and moved away.

"I want his cherry," Dean said, fingers still buried inside him. "It was my sister who found him for us."

"Yes, go ahead. You can have it first. Here," he heard Robert say. Elliot looked over to the left and saw him standing at the end of the bed. Then he tossed something over him to Dean.

Dean leaned over his back and put his hands on Elliot's shoulders, his hardness pressing against his ass through his jeans. "You scared?" he growled, thrusting his hips into him.

"leese, no," he whimpered through the gag.

"Nah, be a good boy, and I'll take the gag off. It won't matter because no one can hear you where we are even if you scream bloody murder." Elliot could feel him keenly, and he couldn't help the fact that his own cock was throbbing worse right then. As scary as this should have been, as frightening as it was, he couldn't help how incredibly hard he was.

Elliot shut his eyes again and felt Dean stand up. He heard the zipper of his jeans. Elliot panted, his heart hammering in his chest. This was it. Dean was really going to do it. He was going to put his cock inside him. Just like all those videos he'd watched and masturbated to. He heard a snapping sound of a bottle opening, and then something cold dripped down the seam of his ass, making him jerk in surprise. He felt Dean's cock pressing against him, sliding against the outside until he pushed in enough to breach him with the tip. Elliot tensed, gasping at the strange feeling of pain and pressure.

"God dammit, relax, fuck," Dean growled. Then he pulled back, sliding completely out for a second before sliding forward again until fully sheathed. This time he seemed to slide in easily. Elliot's eyes flew open at the feeling of something that size going into him. He was obviously not small in any fashion.

"That's tight," Dean commented, tossing something onto the bed. Elliot turned his head to the right and saw it was a bottle of the clear stuff. The bed moved, and Elliot saw David was still sitting at the head of the bed. He got up on his knees to reach over and picked up the bottle before tossing it to the side.

"Don't take all night to get yer nut off," David muttered. "I think I'm gonna play with his mouth some."

Elliot shook his head, feeling Dean slowly thrusting into him. David reached behind his head and untied the gag, pulling it off. Elliot gasped for air, feeling tears hot on his cheeks.

"Please, stop!" he begged.

Instead of stopping, Dean only got a bit faster, and David grabbed him by the hair to jerk his head back. "Now, you bite; you don't get out of here alive, understand?" David told him.

Elliot believed him. Dean grabbed his bound forearms with one hand and his shoulder with the other to pull him until he was standing enough so that David could reach his face. David moved up to him and pulled himself out of the jeans he was wearing, and pressed his cock up against his lips. Elliot opened slightly, and David snapped his hips, shoving himself deep into his mouth and throat. Elliot gagged, choking somewhat on him because he was not small either.

"Do a good job, or you're going to be sucking Dean's cock after he's done fucking your ass," Robert commanded from nearby.

"Good positioning!" Angelica announced before snapping a few more pictures.

Elliot couldn't concentrate on anything except the cock in his mouth and the one filling his ass. Finally, he figured out how to breathe around him, taking heavy breaths through his nose when he pulled back before shoving forward again. He felt his stomach try to rebel and almost thought he would vomit up everything he'd eaten at dinner, but he managed to stop it before it happened.

"If you puke on me, you're going to be so sorry," David admonished as he gripped his hair tighter.

Elliot didn't know how long it had been since they started fucking him, but it felt like forever. Though it felt better than he had ever dreamed, he could feel himself dripping continuously. Then, suddenly, Dean leaned over him again, thrusting hard and sliding a hand from his arms underneath him to grab his cock.

"He's leaking like crazy," Dean said, and Elliot felt his face heat up. He had to be harder than he'd ever been in his life.

"I think he likes it," Robert snarked. "Finish up so he can service me."

"Yeah, yeah, I'll bust my nut soon enough," Dean growled, fucking into him harder than before.

Tears were streaming down his face constantly, and he couldn't stop them as David grabbed his head with both hands and shoved it down into his throat with a grunt. Elliot felt the cock throb in his throat as he came. When David pulled out, Elliot coughed to try to clear his airway and felt something dripping from his mouth. Behind him, Dean seemed to be getting closer because he was ramming into him hard enough that he was shaking the bed. Elliot flexed his hands in their binding and let out a ragged moan.

"Ya sound like a bitch in heat." Dean continued jerking him off.

The words sent him over the edge, and he screamed as he came unexpectedly. Dean paused, wiping his dirty hand on Elliot's lower back, then thrust a couple more times until he slammed into him hard, and Elliot could feel the pulsing of his cock as he came too. Finally, he pulled out, slapping his ass hard as he stepped back.

"Bring him here," Robert said. Elliot glanced over to see that he was sitting in the chair again. Elliot had missed entirely when Robert had moved away from the foot of the bed. His head was not entirely clear, so that he couldn't be sure of anything.

Using the ropes and shirt around his forearms, Dean yanked Elliot to his feet and led him, stumbling over to Robert. "On yer knees, slut."

Elliot fell to his knees without much thought. Robert grabbed his hair and forced his length into his throat until he struggled to breathe, then let him up enough to get a breath before shoving him back down on again. Elliot saw the camera flash again and knew Angelica was still taking pictures. He didn't know how long he was used by Robert, being forced up and down, but eventually, Robert tightened his hold on his hair and forced his head down all the way, sliding his cock down his throat and coming. Robert yanked him off and shoved him back, making Elliot lose his balance and fall to the floor onto his sore ass. He felt someone's legs stop him from falling further and looked up to see Dean standing behind him. He blinked, somewhat dazed, and turned back toward Robert, who was staring at him from where he sat in the chair.

"Not bad for a newbie," Robert told him, dragging a hand through Elliot's now mussed hair.

Tommy came forward as Dean stepped back, and Tommy grabbed him by the forearms and dragged him up to his feet. He pulled him back to the bed, where he fell onto his stomach again. "You're not done yet, princess."

"No, no more, please..." he whimpered. Tommy shoved at his ass, growling at him to get on the bed. Instead, Tommy climbed on to sit at the head where David had been sitting earlier. Elliot didn't move from the position he'd fallen.

"Come here. You better not make me repeat it."

Elliot got up on his knees and moved toward him. As soon as he was close enough, Tommy grabbed him by the arm to pull him toward him to straddle his lap.

"Bottle?" Tommy asked, and David tossed it to him. Elliot had no idea when David had moved over to the side of the bed like that, but he was having trouble keeping track of everyone.

Elliot now realized the bottle was lube. At least they are using lube, he thought as Tommy poured some on his hand and slicked his cock. Tommy grabbed his hips to move him so he was hovering over him.

"You're going to ride, and you're going to do it well, or we're going to shove two cocks up your ass at the same fucking time." Elliot gulped, thinking there was no way that was anatomically possible.

Tommy positioned him, and Elliot felt the head at his entrance. Elliot supposed this position was technically giving him control, but he didn't feel in control of anything. Elliot lowered himself slowly. It must have been too slow for Tommy because he thrust his hips into him sharply. Elliot whimpered as he felt his cock shove the rest of the way into him. He didn't know exactly how to ride someone, so he tried his best. After a few minutes of slowly riding him, Tommy growled and dumped him over on his back, slamming into him without pulling out. Elliot groaned at the odd position since he was lying on his arms. Tommy lifted his legs and rested them over his forearms. Elliot felt his cock against his stomach, leaving stickiness behind, and realized his arousal had returned in full.

"This slut is already hard again," Tommy snarled as he thrust into him harshly.

"What kinda guy gets off on getting raped by four guys?" Dean said from the other side of the bed.

Elliot felt his face flush red, and he turned away, only to have it grabbed and yanked back to face Tommy again. "Don't look away, bitch. I'm not done with you yet." Tommy started brutally slamming right into the spot, which felt really good every time he thrust in and out.

By that point, he was moaning pretty much nonstop. Elliot gasped as he suddenly orgasmed only from being fucked in the ass. Tommy grunted and thrust into him several times before shooting inside him. After a second, he pulled out, leaving Elliot with the sensation of fluid dripping out of him. He thought they were done. They had to be done.

"I haven't had his ass yet," David said, getting Elliot's attention.

David was standing beside the bed, apparently having been there the whole time. He leaned over, grabbed Elliot by the leg near the ankle, and spun him toward him. Then he reached out and rolled him over to his stomach, leaving his legs dangling off the bed.

Before his mind could register what was happening, he plunged into him with surprising ease. Again, he whimpered as David fucked him, but this time he was doing his ass. Everything felt so amazing and good as he felt him repeatedly moving in and out of him. Elliot didn't want David to stop. He saw the flash again out of the corner of his eye. How many pictures had she taken so far? He didn't know or care; he just wanted them to keep fucking him because he couldn't think straight.

"He's gonna get off again if you keep fucking him like that," he heard Dean say, and he was right. Elliot whined as he noticed his cock rubbed against the sheets and was hard once more.

"This bitch loves to be fucked. Such a cock whore," David said as he thrust into him harder and faster.

"I've never seen a slut take this many dicks and still be able to get off on it," Dean laughed.

Elliot felt David come inside him then, leaving his arousal throbbing and pressing between his belly and the sheets. David flipped him over on his back and laughed. "Look at this; he's still dripping."

Elliot moaned as David began stroking him. He knew he wouldn't be able to last very long at the rate things were going. He couldn't believe he'd already gotten off twice and was almost there a third time. He'd never ever been able to orgasm so many times before. Then, David leaned over and sucked Elliot into his mouth. Elliot's eyes went wide, and he gasped at the sensation of his mouth on him. It wasn't his first blow job; he'd had girls do it before, but this felt different. Hotter and more...something. He couldn't name it, but there was something there. He nearly screamed when he came into David's mouth.

Honestly, his mind was completely blank. Everything blurred together, and the world disappeared; he couldn't think, he couldn't move, he couldn't do anything.

But the strangest thing happened. He felt someone untie his arms, and Elliot was wrapping them around whoever was nearest to him, clutching them desperately. He was still panting for breath and hurt in so many places; he felt utterly amazing.

"There, now, yer all right," he heard, and it sounded like Dean.

"Have you got him?" That was Robert's voice.

"Yeah, you can head home; we'll take care of him," came David's voice from the other side of him.

"Call if you need anything," Tommy said, and he heard the door open and close.

"I'll leave you alone," Angelica whispered, and another bright camera flashed behind his eyelids.

Elliot had no idea what was happening, but he needed something he couldn't name. He whimpered as he felt his arms tighten around him. Then, he felt someone's fingers thread through his hair.

"There's a good boy," he heard, feeling hot breath on his ear from behind. "You did so well! Everything was intense, and you were wonderful."

"Yeah, you did good, just like we knew you would." That was Dean's voice from in front of him.

He realized he was still crying, but it wasn't like he was in pain or frustrated; it felt entirely different than before. Now he just felt warm and like the tears were draining everything negative away. He felt something soft against his naked skin and the warmth of the other bodies where they clutched him tightly. He felt soft kisses on the back of his neck and upper back and against his face and throat, and it felt good. The hands gently stroking down his sides and through his hair were so comforting. He couldn't explain how he felt, but it was blissful and relaxing.

"I think he's going to fall asleep before he comes out of it," David's voice sounded far away behind him.

"It's okay if you need to sleep, Elliot," Dean told him. "We'll take care of everything, don't worry. You're safe and taken care of right now."

Elliot felt his mind starting to blank out like he was falling asleep, but he was still keenly aware of the sensations of his body. Every ache and pain was amplified, but instead of being something bad, it only served to remind him how good he was right then. He sighed, tightening his grip on who he guessed was Dean, and nuzzled his face into his warmth. Suddenly, he had to sleep right then and fell into a deeper and more dreamless sleep than he'd ever had.

Sometime later, he woke up feeling comfortable and warm. He wasn't sure what time it was, but he felt like he'd slept for quite a while. At first, he couldn't remember what had happened; as he started moving around, his sore body reminded him keenly of what had gone on the night before. Finally, his eyes flew open, and he slowly sat up. He was in the bedroom in Angelica's house. He'd been cleaned up, and someone had dressed him in pajamas. He saw his clothes neatly hung on the hook behind the door. He got up very slowly because of the pain and changed clothes.

He opened the door and smelled food, causing his stomach to growl in hunger. He swallowed and followed the hallway to the kitchen, where Angelica was busy setting plates on the table. She looked up as he came into the room.

"Come on, sit down. You are probably hungry," she said and indicated a chair. She sat down a plate with bacon, eggs, and toast.

It was like a dream world as he sat down. He jerked and adjusted slightly from the pain as he tried to get comfortable in the chair. He looked at the plate of food and a cup of tea and then at her. She was wearing a set of flannel pajamas, and she had no makeup on like the night before. Instead, she acted like everything was normal, as if he hadn't experienced what he did last night in this house.

"The boys will be back in a minute," she told him as he realized three other plates were set out.

He heard talking coming from the hallway and saw Dean and David chatting.

"Are you going to the Blues game this week?" Dean asked, hands shoved in the pockets of his jeans as he walked.

"Nah, couldn't get tickets and didn't wanna bother Robert about it," David replied.

They both turned to Elliot and smiled as they paused by the table. "Good morning, sweetheart," Dean said.

Elliot thought the whole thing was too surreal after what happened last night. Then it dawned on him.

"You're all from the Real Fantasies Forums, aren't you?" he asked, glancing over to see Angelica smiling at him from across the table. He cleared his throat, realizing it was sore, and his voice sounded rough.

"Ah, I knew you were a smart one last night while we were out and about. You were even smart enough to let me prattle on everything without interruption. That's a rarity I find with men," Angelica told him and gestured to the cup of tea. "Now, drink your tea. It has honey and will help your throat."

Dean sat down next to him and David across from Dean. Dean picked up his fork and looked over at Elliot. "Yeah, Robert runs the forums. He usually don't get involved in the fun, but your message intrigued him, and he wanted to come to join us."

"So, it was all an act," Elliot mumbled, somewhat amazed at everything.

"Of course, you don't think we'd actually force someone against their will, do you?" David said, around a mouthful of food.

"So, whose house is this?" Elliot asked.

"Oh, it's my house," Angelica said, sitting down. "I just took you to the spare room I use when someone's over. We've planned this ever since we found you on the dating app and put together that you were the same person. You listed your email address publicly, and in your fantasy response, you said you liked to use that dating app to meet girls."

"Yeah, you rambled on quite a bit, you know. One of the more detailed responses Robert's ever gotten. Usually, they're just like, 'I want to be raped by a stranger,' and that's it. But, instead, you went all out." David smiled at him.

"So, this Robert, he runs the forum and reads all those requests?" Elliot asked, eating slowly as he spoke.

"Yeah, he's a big-shot CEO of Reid Productions, but he's always been interested in people and sex. I've known him for a couple of years because I'm an intern at his office building here in St. Louis," Dean explained. "David, here is my roommate, and one day we happened to find out about what Robert did on the side."

"How in the world did you do that?" When Elliot thought about it, his eyes went wide.

"David, here's a computer whiz. He hacked into the website and found out who hosted it, and we got caught. But, to our surprise, Robert wasn't really pissed so much as impressed David got around his security," Dean smirked.

"Yeah, I work for him now, too, because he hired me on the spot to help with his cyber security," David said, shoveling a forkful of eggs into his mouth. "I'm finishing my master's program in computer science here at UMSL this year."

"And I really am a photographer for a local magazine," Angelica told him. "I do photo shoots regularly for some amazing models in the area. And I got some phenomenal shots last night."

Elliot's face reddened. "You did? What are you going to do with them?"

"Oh, I thought you'd like something to commemorate the event, so I will assemble a memory book for you. It will be lovely!" she said with a grin, putting down her fork and standing up. She picked up her and David's now empty plates.

"I want another egg, sis," Dean piped up. "If you will, please," he said, giving her a pouty look.

She sighed dramatically. "I guess." She turned and went back to the stove again.

"Why does Robert run the forum?" Elliot was curious about how it all worked.

"He enjoys it more than anything. Plus, now and again, he gets a hookup with someone. His wife doesn't care; she's got her own boyfriend on the side whom he knows about. They have an open marriage, so they both play around," David explained.

"Yeah, and he likes to make people happy, especially those with out-there fetishes. He knows it's hard for those people to get them fulfilled. But David and I often do board requests for him and Tommy. Tommy's Robert's nephew, actually, and he also works for Reid Productions," Dean said, smiling as Angelica plopped another hard-fried egg down on his plate. "Thanks, sis! You're the best."

"Did you get enough to eat, honey?" she asked Elliot. "I can make another egg for you, too, if you want."

"Oh, no, I'm fine! Honest. Thank you so much for the food," Elliot said as he passed his dishes over to her. He cleared his throat again, still somewhat hoarse despite the tea.

She took it and nodded. "All right, as long as you got enough to eat."

"You go to school?" Dean scarfed down his egg.

"Yeah, I go to UMSL, too. I'm in the nursing program." Elliot crossed his arms over his chest and nodded at him.

"That's cool. So, how long you have a fantasy about being gang raped?" David asked, leaning back into his chair with a grin.

Again, Elliot felt his face flush. "Well, it started a while ago when this roommate of mine showed me a video, telling me it was sick and twisted and stuff, but I really liked it. So after that, I started looking for videos and images online, and then I found the forum linked under a video I watched."

"Huh, I always ask," David commented. "And I get all kinds of answers. What video was it, if you don't mind me asking?"

"Oh, it was this video of a bunch of guys in an alley. The one being fucked had this big tattoo down his side, and one of the other guys had ashen, blond hair that was long. He had some tattoos too, and both of them had pierced dicks. I'd never seen anything like that before." Elliot blushed a little remembering the video he still had saved on his phone. It was a favorite, after all.

Elliot noticed that David and Dean looked at each other with a smirk. He was about to say something, but Angelica spoke up first.

"Oh, Terri and I are going down to Strawberry's this weekend; you boys want to come?" Angelica asked as she stretched her arms above her.

"Yeah, we haven't been in a while," Dean said, finishing his egg and passing the plate to his sister.

"Strawberry's?" Elliot asked.

"Yeah, it's a goth club and Dungeon called Strawberry's Black. Fucking amazing place. They allow nudity and sex in the club so that it can get interesting," David grinned at him.

"Sounds like an interesting place." Elliot looked down at his hands for a minute. Then, when no one said anything, he looked up again. "I'm just... I don't know what to say, but thank you for my life's most intense and amazing night."

"Y'know, don't have to be a one-time thing." David winked at him. "I certainly had fun with you last night, and you cry so pretty. Maybe you can even go to the club with us."

Elliot blushed to his roots and looked back down. He nodded slowly. "Okay," he whispered.

And it wasn't a one-time thing at all.

# Double Vision

# A Chains of Fate Story

Jude Hunter looked in the mirror at himself and nodded. He looked good, and he needed to look good today. He was planning on asking the cute barista out. Well, he and his roommate Logan Stone were, anyway. They were looking for a third in their triad. He ran a hand through his chin length blond hair and straightened the rock band t-shirt he was wearing. He'd paired it with a pair of dark jeans and a set of boots he thought looked good. Granted, she'd seen him every day for practically the last month. Today would be the first time he took Logan to the place to see if she was interested in a three-person relationship.

Logan appeared in the doorway. "You're such a princess about what you wear," he groused, arching a black brow at him, brown eyes twinkling.

"I am not!" Jude sighed. "I'm just nervous, is all. You know how this usually goes, and she's probably going to be like all the rest. One guy is fine, but when you mention two, they get skittish."

"Well, it is intimidating. I'm telling you, the guy at the dojang is the one we should ask. He gives us both a look now and then, so I bet he's either gay or bi." Logan sighed and motioned for Jude to hurry up.

Jude frowned. "I mean, yeah, but that girl comes to see him all the time. We've got a better shot with this girl. At least, I think so."

Jude and Logan had been in a relationship for a couple years now, and they'd been looking for a bottom, and possibly a sub if they were into that sort of thing. Jude and Logan were both tops, and neither would give when it came to bottoming, so they had been limited to a few jerk-off sessions, and a blow job or two. Even then, they felt weird about it. They wanted someone they could share between them, and maybe just have to be theirs and no one else. They didn't say it often, but they loved each other quite a bit, and it pained them that they couldn't satisfy each other's needs. Both were bi, well, Logan was pansexual, and Jude just called himself "whatever" and went for what he liked, which Logan kept telling him was being pansexual. Jude didn't feel the need to label himself though.

"Her name's Rose. She's cute as a button, too. Long, shapely legs, feminine in the extreme. I don't think I've seen her wear anything but a dress or skirt since I've been going in. She's always got her hair and makeup done, so she probably would be high maintenance if we hooked up with her. But I'm okay with that," Jude said, running his fingers through his hair again. "Okay, let's go."

They headed out to Jude's small SUV and made their way to the coffee shop. It was a small chain in St. Louis called the Daily Grind, and it was far cheaper and better than the big chains anyway. They pulled in and found it to be not terribly busy, so they got out and headed inside. Jude led, and Logan trailed behind him, looking around as he walked. He liked coffee, but he was usually at the more expensive places. Logan's black hair was sticking out at all angles, Jude noted as he walked in, but then it was usually that way.

As usual, the object of Jude's interest was standing at the counter and smiled at them as they entered. She was dressed in a short sundress that showed off her tanned skin and slender figure. She didn't have much in the way of a bust, but Jude didn't mind that at all. She had cotton candy pink hair that cascaded over her shoulders in gentle waves. The color stood out against her yellow and white dress. Her big, dewy brown eyes sparkled as they approached. Her nametag read "Rose".

"You again?" Rose said softly, and Jude was just amazed at how soft her voice was. If it were any louder in the room, you couldn't hear it. It was a little husky he noticed, but that didn't matter. He thought it was rather sexy.

"Yeah, brought my friend, Logan, to meet you. Er, have coffee," Jude stammered. He bit the inside of his lip. He was being careless.

She smiled again and nodded. "What'll it be?"

"I'll have my usual," Jude said.

"Regular with two sugars?" she said.

"You got it," he nodded. He turned to Logan. "She always remembers."

"And you?" she asked Logan.

"Uh, I'll have a café latte, double sweet."

She nodded and turned around to get it.

Logan glanced at Jude. "Don't she look familiar to you?" Logan muttered softly.

"I just know her from here," he said in a near whisper, looking over the counter at her.

Her dress came to mid-thigh, and Jude was very interested in her shapely legs. They were thicker than most women he knew, but he found them enticing. He had some images of what he would like to do with those legs. She turned back and he lifted his eyes quickly, so she didn't notice him staring. She handed him his drink and he took a moment to touch her hand. She blinked, glancing over at him, and her face reddened a little.

"So, you work here long?" Jude asked. "I don't think I ever asked before."

She shrugged. "Last year or so, you know. I'm going to school at UMSL. My business degree."

She fixed Logan's drink and handed it off to him with a grin. "There you are."

Jude gestured to Logan. "We were wondering if you'd like to go out with us."

Rose blinked. "What?"

"Well, we have a relationship and are looking for someone to date."

"Both of you?" Rose asked, blushing a bit.

Logan sipped the latte. "It ain't common, I know, but we would love it if you'd come out with us, at least see what you think. No pressure, just dinner or something."

A shorter man with dark hair and almond shaped eyes came up beside Rose and stared at them. "Uh, is there a problem here?"

"Oh, no, uh, Darnell. These two just asked me out, I just didn't know how to respond," she told him, looking over and blinking her eyes rapidly.

Darnell arched a brow. "Well, that's up to you, love. Sounds like a fun little proposition."

"With two men?" she asked, still looking a little abashed.

"Seen people with more partners before," Darnell shrugged. "It's called a polycule, and there's a lot of fun to be had with it. Why not give it a try? If you like them, that is," Darnell elbowed her in the side. "If you don't like them, tell them no and leave it at that."

She was still blushing when she turned back. "I mean, I guess just going out would be okay?"

"How about tomorrow night? We can pick you up here, if you'd like, after work?" Jude said with a smirk.

Rose cleared her throat and looked at Darnell, who shrugged. "You're working tomorrow and get off at six when we close, so go for it, love," he said.

"Oh, um, alright, I guess we could go out. Just to see what it's like," she said, and Jude thought her little smile was adorable.

"Are you sure you don't want to ask Peter out?" Logan asked as they got out at the dojang the next morning.

"He's not going to go for it. That girl, Ashley, comes by all the time to see him. And you know he's probably straight," Jude said with a shrug.

"Well, there's no real telling unless we ask him," Logan said, reaching for the door.

They walked into the dojang where the Tae Kwon Do classes were setting up for the morning and saw Peter and Laila were both there. Peter was taller than Laila, who was a short, blond woman who had the capability to take out men twice her size. Master Ryuk hadn't been around lately, but last they heard, he'd gone to visit South Korea.

"I still can't shake the feeling Rose is familiar somehow," Logan said as he sat down to stretch.

"I dunno, maybe. She's a hot little number, though," Jude said with a shrug. "I got a weakness for tall women."

"Let's focus on the workout, Jude, not women!" Laila said, thumping him on the back of the head.

"I sure haven't got a weakness for the short ones," he growled, glaring at her as she moved on down the line.

Logan chuckled and shook his head. The class went well, Laila yelling and Peter coming around and being helpful. He was a black belt and one of the reasons Jude had even gotten involved in the damn class was because he liked the way he moved and looked. Though, as often as that woman came and saw him, he bet there was something going on there.

"Alright, everyone, good job today!" Peter called out, voice loud and strong.

Peter was about Jude and Logan's height, maybe a little shorter, and had close cropped brown hair. He helped a little kid with something up front, then came back toward them. He smiled as he approached.

"Hey, glad to see you guys," came Peter's voice.

"Hey, Peter, how's it going today?" Logan asked, putting his towel in his bag and looking up.

Peter shrugged, smiling at them. Jude was suddenly struck by that same familiarity that Logan was talking about. He didn't know where it came from, but it was there, nonetheless. He shook it away.

"Ah, hey, was wondering if you were busy this weekend?" Jude asked suddenly.

Peter blinked and Logan narrowed his eyes at Jude. "Huh?"

"Like, to do something, maybe go out," Jude continued glancing over at a confused looking Logan.

"Go out?" Peter looked at him, then at Logan. "With you?"

"Well, both of us," Jude said, tilting his head toward Logan. "It's a two-person deal, I guess you could say."

Laila slapped Peter on the ass, startling him. "Why not? You aren't busy."

"Laila!" Peter said, reaching back to cover his ass with both hands. "Um, I've got something to do tonight," he said, and Jude saw that he was blushing.

"Tomorrow's good," Logan said, shrugging.

"Oh, I guess," he said. "Um, give me your number, and I'll text you tomorrow."

"Okay," Jude said, reaching out for Peter's phone.

Peter handed it over and Jude had to do a double take because he had a sparkling purple case on the phone. It even had a pop socket with a unicorn on it. He didn't say anything, though, just put his number in the contact section, but he did note the Pegasus on the phone background. He handed the phone back to him and he turned and disappeared. Laila was giving them a grin, though, before she turned and went to the front of the room.

"What do I do?" Peter said as he sat in the office at the Ryuk Dojang.

Master Ryuk was Darnell's father, and in his absence, Darnell ran the place, though he was no martial artist. Instead, he let Peter and Laila run the classes along with a few other of his father's students. Darnell much preferred to run his coffee shop than the dojang.

Darnell stared at him and shook his head. "Only you would get a date with the same two guys twice in as many days."

"But I'm going with them tonight as Rose. Then they want me to go out as Peter. So, what the hell do I do? Do I tell them I'm the same person?" Peter put his head in his hands and didn't know what he was supposed to do.

"Well, since they're into both your female and male sides, that's a good sign they might be a good fit for you all around," Darnell said.

"But how do I explain that I'm bigender and switch between the two modes?" Peter sighed.

"Just like that. I mean, what happens if things go really well tonight, and they end up wanting to take you to bed? Are you just going to be like, surprise! By the way, I'm the same person you tried to ask out at the dojang today." Darnell shrugged. "I mean, just tell them tonight who you are. I mean, that blond one has been coming into the Daily Grind for the last year, and I'm sure it's because of you. And honestly, he's also had his eye on you as Peter since he started coming here. The dark-haired one, I don't know much about him, but he seems to be as interested as his friend."

Laila came in and flopped beside him on the sofa. "Confused about being asked out?" she asked.

"Yeah. You weren't there, but they also asked me out as Rose at the coffee shop."

"Well, ain't that perfect? They want to fuck both of you."

Peter slapped her on the leg and sighed because she had such a vulgar mouth sometimes. "Alright, I'll just go tonight and see what happens. I've gotta get dressed for work at the coffee shop anyway, so might as well be ready for tonight," he said, standing up.

"Wear something slutty," Laila called as he went out the door.

How was he going to explain himself to these two? He didn't know. He'd dated guys as Rose before, but never more than one or two, and he'd dated women as Peter, but they never lasted. He'd yet to be asked out by a guy as Peter, so that was new to him. He headed to his small apartment he shared with his friend Anita. He came in and stood at the door until she popped out of the kitchen. She was a muscular woman herself, a weightlifter, actually. She had short, red hair and light green eyes to go with it. As a matter of fact, she was going to do some competitive weightlifting in the next couple weeks.

"Something wrong? Don't you have to get ready for the coffee shop?" she asked, wiping her hands on a towel.

"I got asked out after work. By a pair of guys that are together." He paused and looked up. "Then the same two guys asked me out at the dojang."

Anita arched a brow and smiled. "Sounds like it might be the right match for you."

"But they don't know Rose and Peter are both me," Peter said, standing up and coming into the apartment further. "What if it weirds them out? I mean, I know it's not exactly normal, but it is what I am..."

"Peter, don't worry until it comes to that. Just go out and have fun, then if it comes down to it, tell them the truth. They'll either accept you as you are, or they won't. Either way, you'll know whether they're right for you or not." Anita smiled and came over to him, hugging him. "Just either way, be you, and if they don't like it, they're not right for you."

So, after work, Rose waited nervously for Logan and Jude to arrive. Darnell stood with her and waited, having come back to the Daily Grind just to make sure she got off on her date fine. She'd gone with a short, flirty skirt that flared out around her legs, and a frilled shirt that showed off the small bust she had underneath it. She didn't have a lot to work with but inserts and a pushup bra did wonders. She was about to write it off as being a farce when there was a knock at the door. It was after close, so they couldn't just walk in.

"There you go, love. Have fun!" Darnell said. "And be careful. If they try anything you don't want, beat their asses, got it?"

Rose hugged him back. "Okay, I will."

She walked out and saw them both leaning against the outside of the small SUV they were in. Jude stood up and came forward, pulling a small bouquet of pink flowers. She smiled, taking them, and sniffing them.

"Oh, thank you!" she said.

Logan gestured to the front seat, so she climbed in, careful of her skirt. Jude shut the door and went around to the driver's side and got in. Logan got in behind her.

"Figured we'd go for dinner and a movie, what do you think?" Logan said from the back.

"Sounds wonderful," she said, smiling broadly.

They pulled into a Randy's Diner, which she was glad of. She knew that she'd be able to find something to eat there and it would be a reasonable praice as well. She worried about who was going to pay, but she'd brought her wallet with her just in case they paid separately. She didn't want to assume anything like they were paying for her or anything. They got out and she slung her purse around her and walked in beside them.

"Three today?" the host asked as they walked in.

"Yes, please," Logan said with a nod.

"Table or booth?" she asked as she picked up the menus and silverware.

Logan looked at Jude and then her. "Ah, we'll have a table, I think."

The host nodded and led them to a square table. She sat down and Jude sat on one side of her, while Logan sat on the other. She settled into her seat and took the menu from the host and opened it.

"I haven't been to Randy's in a while," she said, looking over the menu.

"We come here sometimes after we go to a local club on the weekends," Jude said.

"What can I get you to drink?" a server said as she came up to the table.

"Ah, I'll have sweet tea," Jude said.

"Diet cola," Rose said, nodding.

"And I'll have a regular cola." Logan didn't look up as he ordered it.

"Gotcha," the server, Sue, her name tag read, said.

Rose quickly found what she wanted. A chicken Caesar salad. She hadn't had one in a while, and it seemed like a good choice. Plus, it was reasonably priced. She closed the menu and looked up as the server brought their drinks and sat them down.

"Ready to order?" she asked, looking around at each of them.

"I am, what about you two?" Logan said.

"Yeah, I'm good, you Rose?" Jude closed his menu, too.

"Yes, I'll have a chicken Caesar salad, please," she said, nodding at her.

Logan spoke up next. "I think I'll have the soup and sandwich, a French dip and broccoli cheddar soup."

"And I'll just have a cheeseburger and fries, please, no tomatoes." Jude closed his menu and collected the other two to hand over to the server.

"Sounds good, I'll have it out for you soon," Sue said and turned and headed to the kitchen.

"So, first date, and all, figure we should get to know each other," Jude said, sipping his tea.

Rose felt her face heat up a little, so she ducked her head a bit and took a drink of her soda. She cleared her throat and wondered how she was going to do this. She couldn't tell them the things she liked to do as Peter. So, she guessed she would stick to things they didn't know about Peter.

"Well, I like to write," she said, looking between them.

Jude arched a brow. "Really? What kind of stuff do you like to write?"

She smiled, a little embarrassed but willing to talk about her hobby. "Oh, poetry and fantasy. I really like reading high fantasy and that's my favorite thing to write. You know, sword and sorcery and knights and stuff."

"Really?" Logan said, running a hand through his dark hair. "You'll have to show us something you've written."

"Oh, I don't know if I could do that," she chuckled. "I mean, I have a book of poems I put together, but no one has ever bought it to read..."

"You mean you self-published it?" Jude said, leaning forward a bit. "That's awesome!"

"Yeah, you should be proud of that! It's quite the accomplishment," Logan smiled at her.

She felt her cheeks burning by now. "Yeah, but what about you guys? What do you like to do?"

They glanced at each other, then Jude spoke up first. "Well, I like sports. A lot of them, and I weight lift about three times a week. I really like wrestling and want to be a professional. But that's a pipe dream, probably, you know, so I go to school to be a history teacher so I can coach high school wrestling."

Rose noticed he didn't mention the martial arts class. Probably for the best, she thought. She already knew how muscular Jude was, just from watching him in class. He had one defined body, and despite what she had thought to start the night out, she kind of wanted to see it naked. She shook the thought away and turned to Logan.

"And you? Are you in sports, too?"

"Well, I'm actually a runner," Logan said. "Cross country. I like to do marathons and stuff like that, but it won't be a career. I'm going to school to be an IT professional. Computers are my thing, really. I'm kind of an introvert and keep to myself most of the time. Guess that's why I leave it to Jude to bring up dating."

"So, how did you two meet, and like, hook up?" she asked, looking between them.

"Ha, that's a funny story," Jude said, smirking. "See, I was looking for a roommate a couple years ago when I started out at the university. I was about to put an ad up on the posting board when this guy tapped my shoulder to ask if I was putting up an ad. I said yeah, and then we got to talking a bit, and found out we were in the same year, and both of us were from little rural towns outside St. Louis, so we thought we'd take on the big city together."

"Yeah, but how did you get together?" she asked, leaning forward.

Logan looked at Jude and cleared his throat. He blushed a little and leaned closer to her.

"Ah, well, we'd been living together for a while and went out drinking one night. We both got pretty hammered, and when we got home, some stuff started happening, and before it got too far, we both realized we were tops, and neither one of us was willing to bottom. So, we, ah, ended up jerking each other off, and things went from there. That's when we started looking for a third." He spoke the last in a near whisper so as not to be overheard by those around them.

She nodded, understanding that. If neither was willing to bottom, but they still wanted to be in a relationship, that would severely limit their sex life. "So, do you still do stuff like that?"

"Well, yeah," Jude said, looking around to make sure no one was listening to closely to them. He was still talking very quietly though. "I mean, we'll mess around, just not the actual sex, you know."

"It's unconventional," Logan said, giving her a wry smile and trying to seem casual. "I mean, I get that. That's why our dates usually don't work. Guys get jealous and don't want to share, and girls get scared off because there's two of us and they feel outnumbered in the situation. So, we get it. We know it isn't the easiest relationship style to be a part of. But right now, we can't meet all of each other's needs."

Rose thought both were being quite candid and honest with her, and she really appreciated that. She wasn't intimidated by them, of course, but she was a third-degree black belt in Tae Kwon Do. She could handle herself, and had no doubt that if they tried anything, she could handle them, too. She looked up and saw the server coming with their food, so they let her set it down and for a few minutes they ate in silence.

"You do anything else besides write and work at the coffee shop?" Jude asked, setting down his cheeseburger.

"Well, yeah, I'm going to the university, too. I'm a business student," she said. She left off the part that she was going to school to help Darnell run both the dojang and the coffee shop. In fact, if things worked out, she was set to take over one of them completely when she finished the business program.

"Business, huh?" Logan said. "Funny, that school is so big, and we've never seen you there," he continued.

She smiled and didn't say anything. She went to school as Peter, so there was no way they would ever have seen her there. Her life at the coffee shop was the only place she got to present as purely female, and it was freeing to even be on a date as Rose. She sipped her drink and wondered what she was going to do as the night came to an end. She knew she'd probably have a choice to make.

"You've got such an aura about you," Jude said, looking at her.

She blinked and tilted her head to the side. "Is that a good thing?"

"Oh, it is, believe me. It's a beautiful aura," he continued.

She felt her cheeks heat up a little and she swallowed. "You're too sweet."

"He's right, though," Logan said. "It's a lovely feeling around you. And it matches your beauty."

She wasn't sure how to respond to that. She dabbed her lips with her napkin and looked away for a second. "I really think I like you both, too."

"Do you?" Logan said, leaning a bit closer. "Because the night's not over yet."

"Ah, yeah, the movie," she said, clearing her throat.

"The movie." Jude said. "Yeah, the movie."

Jude reached over and took her hand gently. "Do you mind?" he said.

She looked down at his hand and shook her head. "Uh, no, it's fine."

"I'm glad," he said, stroking her hand. He rubbed it for a second. "How'd you get those?" he asked, rubbing the slight calluses that she had on her palms. She swallowed thickly, not wanting to reveal they came from her work with various weapons like the bo staff, sai, and swords.

"Ah, just use my hands a lot," she said, pulling back a little, but finding Jude didn't let go.

"Still, they're lovely hands," he said, pulling the back of her hand to his lips.

She swallowed again and felt the blush on her cheeks. He let go of her hand and she put both in her lap. She looked up to see the server had come to bring them refills on their drinks and she was glad of the breather, because the closeness with these two was taking her breath away. She had no idea why, perhaps it was because she already knew them from classes. She couldn't tell them, though.

"Can I take your plates?" Sue the server said as they lapsed into silence.

"Uh, yeah," Rose said and picked up her empty plate to hand over. Jude and Logan did the same.

"Movie?" Jude said as the server walked away.

"Oh, uh, sure. Something interesting. I'm not into sappy romances or boring comedies," she said, then wished she hadn't. That eliminated a lot of the movies they could watch.

Jude glanced over at Logan. "A woman who knows what she wants," he said with a slight smile. "Alright, let's see if we can't find something we'll all enjoy."

It was a blur from the restaurant to the movie theater. Neither of them got too close, but Jude acted like he wanted to take her hand a couple times. She thought it was kind of sweet and would have let him if he had tried. They ended up choosing a new action movie that they were all interested in seeing. Jude insisted on buying drinks and popcorn even though Rose protested that it cost too much for them to get. They found a seat near the back, with Logan on one side and Jude on the other.

About halfway through the movie, Jude put his arm around her, and she leaned a bit into him. Then, Logan slipped one hand over on her knee and then took her hand on that side. It was comfortable, and she smiled, completely focused on them and not the movie. Her heart was hammering in her chest, and she knew where she wanted the night to go. She just worried that when they found out the truth, that she was Peter, too, that they would be disgusted or hateful about it. It was her greatest fear when living the double life she lived.

By the end of the movie, she'd nervously drank her entire soda and had to pee really bad, which she hoped she could get the gaff off in time to go because it was getting urgent. As the credits rolled, she stood up and looked at them.

"I need the bathroom," she said, and headed down the row, leaving them to follow her.

She glanced back and saw they were right behind her, and then she disappeared into the women's restroom. She got into a stall and managed to get the gaff down just in time. She sighed in relief and wondered what would happen now. The two of them seemed to have liked her so far tonight, and if that was the case, then would they invite her back to their place?

She came out of the bathroom to find both standing outside waiting patiently. Jude reached for her hand, then Logan reached for the other. She blushed a little, but she took their hands, and they walked out of the movie theater. They headed across the road to the parking spot, and then both kind of stopped. Jude pulled her close first and hovered over her lips.

"Can I kiss you?" he whispered huskily.

Rose nodded and he pressed into her lips with his, sliding his tongue effortlessly into her mouth. She responded, returning the kiss, and feeling Logan's hand tighten in hers. Then, Jude moved back, and Logan pulled her his direction, smiling a bit and coming close to her lips.

"Can I, now?" he asked, and she nodded again, finding he was gentler, sliding his tongue through her teeth and sucking a bit on her tongue.

He pulled back and both were obviously interested in what they were doing. Rose wasn't doing much better, and she was glad she hadn't worn a tight skirt, because tucking with a hard on didn't work that well.

"I wanna take this back to our place. What do you say?" Jude breathed harshly.

"Okay," Rose said, head fogged with lust at the moment.

They all got in the car, and she almost forgot the most important thing. She had to tell them. But how was she going to do that now? She tried a couple times as they drove, but it didn't come out and she couldn't figure out exactly how she was supposed to tell them the truth. Before she got it figured out, they were back at their place, a small house set back from the road.

Jude got out and opened the door for her. She got out, Logan following her. Jude grabbed her hand and led her into the house.

"Listen, there's stuff you should know," she finally said, not sure if she was going to be able to say it.

"Don't worry about it, just come on. We'll have some fun," Logan said, wrapping an arm around her shoulders and steering her toward what she guessed was the bedroom.

Despite what she said, she didn't try to stop at all. She just kept walking and thinking about what she wanted to say and how she wanted to say it. But these guys were moving fast now that the moment was upon them, and even though she knew she could stop the whole thing, a bigger part of her wanted to continue.

"I mean, I'm serious, we should talk first," she said tentatively as she sat down on the end of the bed. "There's something you should know about me."

Immediately, though, Jude dropped between her legs and slid both hands up her thighs under her skirt. Logan got behind her and began undoing the buttons on her shirt. She felt Jude going for the tight gaff she was wearing, and she saw the confused expression cross his face. Then his hand brushed her trapped erection. He looked up, eyes a bit wider.

"Um, you..."

"I'm sorry, I tried to tell you!" she said, tears collecting at the corners or her eyes.

Logan's hands ran down her chest and found the flat planes instead of the expected curves, and she knew that this was about to go bad. She hadn't gotten it out yet, and now they were going to know everything.

"You've got a dick," Jude said, looking up at her.

She nodded, tears slipping down her face, makeup starting to run. "Yeah, and you've probably guessed, I'm not just Rose, I'm—"

"Peter," Logan said, reaching up and sliding the wig off her head gently.

Jude locked eyes with Logan then shrugged, hands sliding back under the skirt and pulling at the waist of the gaff. "Hey, you got a dick. I know what to do with one of those," Jude said, and managed to pull the gaff down her hips. "Do you want to be called Rose or Peter?"

Now that it was out, Peter dropped out of his Rose persona, and spoke in his voice instead of the practiced feminine voice.

"It doesn't matter," he said, completely thrown off by their casual acceptance of the situation.

"Well, we like both, so there," Logan said, kissing Peter's neck and nibbling on it. "I didn't expect to get both a girl and a boy at one time, but hey, it works. You be whoever you want to be, baby."

A few seconds later, the clothes were discarded and all three of them were in the bed, naked bodies pressed against each other. Peter was lying between Jude and Logan, Jude sliding his hand up and down their cocks where they met and Logan rubbing against his entrance. He hadn't done this in a while, in fact, it wasn't since high school since he'd bottomed for someone. Then, he'd gotten involved with a teacher in an illicit affair that ended up coming out and getting the teacher fired. Peter still regretted getting Dr. Mansfield fired, but he supposed that a man of his age should have known better than to get involved with a teenager.

"I can't wait to fuck you any longer," Logan said, kissing the back of Peter's neck and biting lightly at it. "But let's have a little fun with it."

Peter felt him move off the bed and then return with a bottle of lube and a pair of handcuffs. He looked at him as he took his hands and locked the handcuffs around the headboard slat and slapped them on him. He got between his legs and Jude laid beside him, pinching a nipple and then sucking on it gently.

The bottle clicked open, and he felt Logan slide two fingers into him at once. He gasped, feeling it burn and stretch a little. He opened his legs wider, though, moaning as Jude continued to torment his nipples one at a time. He wanted to use his hands but felt the tug on the handcuffs when he tried.

"Can't wait, ready to go now," Logan said, sliding up and slicking himself with the lube.

"Just go for it," Peter growled. "I won't break!"

"You said it," Logan said, positioning himself and slamming himself forward hard.

"Oh, my gods," Peter gasped, arching and pulling on the handcuffs again as Jude bit down on his nipple.

Logan slid back and forth a few times, finding a rhythm and then speeding up. "Fuck, you're tighter than I expected, but it's been a while since I've done this," Logan said.

Jude, meanwhile, had found Peter's mouth, and was plundering it for all it was worth as Logan fucked him. It took a bit, but eventually he moaned out as Logan began striking his prostate just right, sending sensation all the way to his cock. Jude reached down and stroked him as Logan slammed into him harder and harder. He tightened his legs around Logan and came hard in Jude's hand, giving a minute, and then feeling Logan throbbing inside him as he came too.

Logan pulled out and Jude let go of his mouth, then reached down and flipped him to his stomach. He moved behind him and yanked his hips up.

"Logan's cum is sliding out of you, now I'm going to fill you up some more, okay, babe?" Jude said, lubing himself with the bottle Logan handed him and then sliding himself into him. Peter arched under him, growing hard just from all the stimulation.

"You're a mess," Logan said, as Peter turned his head to the side. "Your makeup is all run down your face, and tears are in your eyes. It makes you beautiful," he said, cupping his face and leaning down to kiss him.

Jude continued and Logan took a turn kissing him. Peter was sure his hips were going to be bruised from the grip Jude had on him, but that was okay. It felt good, and he didn't want him to stop. And the kissing was amazing. He'd never been kissed like this before, and he was feeling it all the way to his toes for the first time. He felt his end rushing at him again, and he moaned out into Logan's mouth.

"I'm not lasting long," Jude said. "I'm going to fill you up, got it, babe? And from now on, you belong to us, and no one else. No one gets to fuck you like this, got it?"

Peter moaned again, nodding as he felt the orgasm crash into him just from Jude's words. He was claimed and he was going to be theirs. They wanted him, just as he was, and that was just fine by him. Jude slammed into him, releasing into him. He pulled out and let go of Peter, who collapsed, the bed under him wet.

"Hey, baby, just a minute, let me let you out," Logan said, reaching for the handcuffs.

A few minutes later, he was cuddled in between them again, and they were both caressing him. He was covered up, the wet spot covered with a convenient towel that was handy and snuggled up comfortably. He'd never felt like this before, and he didn't know what to do about it, to be honest.

"I think I love you already," Jude said softly. "I think I fell in love the first day I saw you, both of you. You're why I took the martial arts classes, and you're why I keep going to the coffee shop."

Peter smiled softly. "I think I liked seeing you in both places. I was surprised you never realized I was the same person."

"Don't leave me out!" Logan said, squeezing him from behind. "I may not have been crushing, but I definitely was on board with it!"

Peter chuckled. "Well, for that, I'm glad."

Peter. Rose. One in the same, really. He thought about it, and as he lay there, snuggled between the two of them, he realized that he was more than either one of them, or even the combination of both his names. He was just who he was, and he'd finally found those that would care for all of him. Her. Both.

# The Corporal and His Contessa

## A Chains of Fate Story

### His Submission

*P*resent

"Don't you dare move one inch," Contessa's voice commanded from behind the Corporal.

The Dungeon was dimly lit, and it was a great comfort to the bound man on his knees before his Domme. Also of great comfort, was their closeness to a nearby couch. Should it become necessary, She would be able to move him on to it. His bad leg was beginning to ache as he held the kneeling position. He sat back on his heels and allowed his weight to rest on the balls of his feet. It was not yet enough that he needed to signal Her. His breath came in pants and he focused on the sensations caused by being bound.

Focusing on his wrists, he felt the pressure from the supple leather cuffs. The cuffs clipped to the D ring on the back of his matching leather collar. It made any move to relax increase the pressure on his neck. The strain on his shoulders and back was pleasant and painful at the same time as he kept his back straight and his elbows out. A slight sheen of sweat had appeared on his skin, and he could feel the sharper twinge of pain that came from the circular scar in his left shoulder. He could hear the slight jingle from the nipple clamp chain that had been fed through the front D-ring in his collar. The clamps themselves were metal clover clamps and the slightest movement increased the pain and pressure, especially if he moved his head or hands. The cool metal bounced against his chest and belly with each breath. His desert camo fatigue shirt hung open and he could keenly feel the soft material brush against the bruises on his back.

Perhaps the most comforting feel was the wide leather belt just below his slightly pudgy belly that wound around his hips. It rested near some of the thicker scars that began at his hips and went downward. Kneeling in this position made the presence of the connecting straps that ran from the belt down the front and sides of his thighs feel tighter. He could sense the scars keenly because the newer flesh was so much more sensitive than the other skin. Where they buckled to the wide leather cuffs at mid-thigh, he could see and feel the flesh puffing above and below them. His bare thighs felt slightly cold, and he glanced toward his folded fatigue pants with his combat boots sitting atop them.

The sight of his uniform forced a sudden series of memories to impinge on his thoughts. There, in the once serene landscape, memories of blood raining down and the sounds of explosions began to replay. He actively fought the feeling of panic rising in his chest. There were a million reasons why this happened, and those were the reasons he knelt here tonight before his Mistress. Once again, this week had been bad for him; one of his best friends was still gone for an unknown amount of time under FBI protection. He and his Mistress were still under the watch of an FBI agent and might be at risk of being a target. All of this brought forward the memories of the battlefield and the feeling of fearing for his life. There was the echo of an explosion in his mind and his pants started to come faster and faster.

Thwack.

Somewhere between the sting of the impact and the sound of the crop his eyes flew open; the explosion and blood faded. He stared at his left thigh where a bright red splotch was beginning to form. The mark was above the point on his leg where the twisted scar tissues covering the left side of his leg began.

"Focus."

That single stern word from Contessa was enough to force everything out of his mind except the current moment. The past faded as the pain transformed the anxiety into something more manageable.

"Yes, Mistress. Yes." He swallowed hard as an identical red mark appeared on his other thigh. "Ahhh," he exhaled slowly.

His Mistress. His everything. He looked up at Her with adoring eyes. Her blonde hair was perfect as always, pulled up into a tight bun. Her back was straight and the riding crop She held seemed to be an extension of Her arm. It drew his focus to the strap of the handle which was adorned with a small gold ball. The black leather of the strap and handle contrasted against the white leather of the elbow-high gloves She wore. Smoothly, She lifted Her arm and snapped the crop down across his left thigh. Another spot of red arose and he felt his cock twitch in the metal chastity device he wore. There was no doubt a puddle was gathering under him because he could feel himself dripping. She would deny him many times when he started begging for release.

When She turned Her back to him, the Corporal was taken by Her sheer beauty. The black leather miniskirt She wore accented the pronounced curve of Her ass and ended just above the lace edged thigh-highs. He could barely see the ends of the straps to Her black garter belt. The white, sheer blouse barely obscured the black lace accented corset She wore under it. He knew Her corset displayed Her breasts prominently. They were dusted with glitter, and he knew and it would taste like raspberries if he were permitted to have a taste.

"How many so far, My slave?" She asked as She turned back to face him.

"Th-three, Mistress." His answer was stuttered from excitement.

Smack. The crop sounded much louder when She slapped it on the table near their scene. "And how many more?" She demanded.

"Seven." The response was immediate and without hesitation. He had earned ten. He wanted ten. He needed ten.

"Good, good." She circled him again. "Shall we continue?" She asked.

He knew She was asking for confirmation; She was ensuring that his leg was still in good enough condition to continue. He knew She would change his position if that was not the case. He had no fear of his Mistress; She would take him as far as he wanted to go and no further.

"Yes, Mistress. Please, Mistress."

*Thwack.*

## His Problem

*Several Months Ago*

"Sasha..." Charles Ruebern couldn't keep the whine out of his voice. "She's gorgeous," he muttered as he planted his face on the surface of the bar.

Beside him was his friend Sasha, a man he'd served under in the army until his discharge. Sasha sat and listened to him go on and on about the waitress he'd seen at her workplace three times in the last two weeks.

"Ask her out, then, and stop being so..." Sasha sighed and ran a hand over his black buzz cut hair before scratching his stubbly chin. Charles knew what he was going to say. Stop being so submissive. But Sasha knew he couldn't help it. "Okay, you are going to have to take a chance, Charles. You can't just let her go if you want her so desperately." He reached over and placed a firm hand on the back of Charles's neck.

Charles sat up immediately with a bit less desperation in his eyes. The weight and pressure of Sasha's hand helped him focus. He took a deep breath as Sasha removed his hand and Charles picked up his beer. "You're right, but you know I don't do well with this part. Carmine would laugh at me. I wish I had his confidence."

Sasha smiled. "Carmine isn't a sub. I know it is not easy for you to take this step, but you must do so. Is she in the Lifestyle?" he asked as he sipped his vodka splashed with green apple liquor. Sasha's voice picked up more of his Russian accent when he was drinking. It always made Charles smile, because he otherwise tried to hide it. Charles turned his head and looked at him.

"I don't think so." He shook his head.

Sasha glanced at him. "Then how is it she's going to satisfy your needs, Charles?"

Swallowing thickly, Charles chewed his lip for a few seconds. "I don't know, but maybe I can recruit her? She's got the markers for being a good Domme. She exudes that presence, and it is so intoxicating."

Sasha sighed again and stared at Charles before smirking and raising his drink in toast. "Udachi, my friend." He took another sip of his drink.

"I don't know how you drink that awful shit. Vodka is bad enough by itself," Charles said before downing the last of his beer as Sasha chuckled.

## His Strength

*One Week Later*

Charles had been back in St. Peters, and once again he was sitting in the all-night diner. He started coming here while working a side job hauling car parts for a small mechanic shop. He ran a lunchtime radio show, but it didn't pay well. He had gotten a side job doing the only other thing he knew best: driving. While in the military, he trained as a Motor Transport Operator. Driving long distances and loading and unloading trucks was something he was used to doing from his time in the military. That made it easy to pick up the part time job for McShoogin's Mechanic Shop. All he had to do was pick up parts shipments in St. Louis and bring them to St. Peters. Since he lived in St. Louis, he got to keep the work van during his off time. Some days he got done early, but others it was well after dark when he got all the parts unloaded finally. The first time he stopped at the local Randy's had been because it was late enough that it had been the only place open.

That first time he'd stopped here, he saw her. She wasn't his waitress then, but a young girl named Janet was. At first, he didn't think much of the tall, buxom blonde bussing some nearby tables. Then, a rowdy patron at the table next to him grabbed Janet's ass and made some rude comment to her.

The other waitress's head lifted and her blue eyes settled on the perpetrator of the comment. A few strides took her from the dirty table she was bussing to where the younger woman stood trying to politely disengage the drunk man's hand from her skirt. One purposeful smooth move, and the other waitress had pulled his hand away.

"Do not touch her again or I'll have you escorted out of the restaurant. Sir."

The man had laughed, but the blonde waitress didn't waver. A few minutes later, he'd been escorted out cursing her and the younger waitress as he went. Charles caught sight of her name tag and saw it read Clair. He smiled to himself as she comforted Janet. After a while, Clair had come and taken over his table. He couldn't do anything except drop a ten-dollar tip and mutter "Thank You."

Over the next month, he had stopped there as often as possible. She waited on his table a few more times. Once he saw her speaking with a very tall, muscular man with multi-colored hair. She had kissed the taller man on the cheek before he left with the young waitress, Janet. Despite being afraid the man might have been her boyfriend, he needed to take this chance to talk to her. Just seeing her made his heart race and it wasn't just her looks. It was in the way she carried herself, and the way she cared for the younger waitress; it all spoke of the type of dominance he was looking for.

After speaking with Sasha, he felt more confident. Being submissive didn't make him weak and he knew it. Nonetheless, it did make this harder. It also didn't help that he had never been very good with women. Carmine was so good with women, and Sasha was already married.

Today had been an early day; the van had only been half full so unloading it hadn't taken very long. It always seemed to take longer than he wanted because he had to break frequently to give his bad leg a rest. He was lucky that he didn't get paid by the hour, instead being paid per trip and the weight of the load. Since he had to take so many breaks, hourly would have gotten him fired.

He found himself hesitating as she came toward the table, but he screwed up his courage enough to speak to her.

"I'm sorry, Miss Clair, but I was wondering if I could ask you a question." He turned his face up to her as she sat down his glass of iced tea.

She looked at him and blinked. "Oh, what is it?" she inquired. Her voice was so lovely. There was a husky tone to it, but it had such strength behind it. It made his stomach flip just being near her, and even as nervous as he was, he just felt calmer around her.

"I imagine you get propositioned a lot in this job by rude men who see you as no more than an object." As soon as the words were out of his mouth he regretted them. That sounded so ridiculous.

The waitress narrowed her gorgeous blue eyes and stared at him before responding. "You would be correct."

"Never mind; this was stupid." Licking his lips in nervousness, he looked away from her and ran a shaking hand over his shaggy brown hair.

A good minute passed before she said anything. He turned back in nervousness to see what she was going to do. Then she gave him a half smile. "Meet me out front after my shift ends at five. We can get coffee if you like."

Charles watched her go in utter shock. He nodded emphatically to himself and left with more confidence than he knew he had.

## His Surprise

*Later That Day*

Five o'clock came around, and Charles stood nervously waiting for her to come out of the diner. He'd gone home and changed out of the grimy work clothes he wore on deliveries. He had returned in nice jeans and a dark blue button up shirt as well as with his own car. Clair came out, still in the clothes she wore at work, only without her apron. Even though it was just a simple black A-line skirt and a white blouse, her presence took his breath away.

"Well, come on, then," she commanded as she walked past him down the sidewalk.

He quickened his steps and caught up to her and instinctually walked behind her. She kept a swift pace and turned into one of those fancy coffee shops that seem to pop up on every corner these days. He followed her inside as she placed her order, then mechanically put in his own order. Once they acquired their drinks and sat down at a table, she looked over her coffee at him.

"So, you wanted to ask me out."

Somewhat in shock that she'd agreed, he nodded. "And you wanted to come out with me. I didn't think you would."

"Maybe I was intrigued."

"I seduced you with my awkwardness?" he asked, giving her a wry smile.

She smiled in return. "Something like that. You haven't even introduced yourself yet, so I would say awkward is an understatement. I know your name is Charles, from your uniform."

Charles reddened immediately. "Oh, God, I forgot. Um, I'm Charles Ruebern. I'm so sorry." He apologized as he reached across the table.

She shook his hand. As expected, Charles found her handshake to be firm and without hesitation. "Clair Jaeger." She grinned at him. "You deliver car parts to McShoogins."

"Yeah, guess you'd say that's my side gig," he sighed as he stared at his hands. "I have this radio show I run during lunchtimes, but it doesn't pay the bills. You know, a work of passion, so I have to do something to make money." He sipped his coffee. "After I got discharged from the army, I spent some time in a bottle, y'know. When I pulled myself out, with my buddies' help, I started doing the radio thing." He blinked, looking up at her. "I'm sorry. That was way over shareing."

Instead of seeming annoyed, Clair smiled. "No, it's okay. I mean, first dates are about sharing, right?"

First date? Charles felt his heart start to pound. That indicated there might be a second. "I guess you're right. I just have never been good with women. My buddy, he's so smooth. I think he can get anyone in bed. I've seen him seduce a dude and a girl at the same damn time..." he muttered morosely.

"That's some talent," she smirked. "He seems like a slick number."

Charles smiled, starting to relax. Talking about someone else was a whole lot easier than talking about himself. "Oh, God, yes. He loves it, though. Well, kind of. He doesn't like having so many lovers, but he hasn't found the one that stuck, y'know? I swear, I wish I had half his ability with women. I don't go for men, so I'll skip that part."

"My big brother doesn't do well with women or men, but it doesn't bother him. He moved back recently after being out in California for a while. He was telling me about a bad experience he had out there. He's not into relationships now, he says. Something I'm not surprised about. I believe he just hasn't dealt with what happened..." she trailed off and sipped her drink.

"Um, that big guy with the blue hair?" he asked, noticing her look of concern. "Oh, that's your brother," he mumbled almost to himself.

"Yeah, Varick," she nodded. "He's a sweetie, a lot rougher looking than he is. He's a big teddy bear. Our father used to call him *Moppelchen* when he was a little boy because he was so chubby."

"*Moppelchen?*"

"Our father's German, I thought the last name gave it away." She gave him an amused grin. "*Moppelchen* means 'little chubb-sie'. Really cute, you know." As she spoke, she swirled the coffee in the paper cup.

Charles smiled again, completely drawn in by her presence. "I don't have any siblings." Charles sighed as he started thinking about the past. "Just me and my dad growing up. Well, and my buddy Carmine. He lived next door to me, and we lived down in what I guess you'd call a questionable neighborhood."

"You said you were in the military? Did you just do one tour or something and get out?"

Shaking his head, he took a breath. "Nah, I was the driver for my company, and we got into a bad spot, a bomb went off and we had to leave the cars." His eyes went distant for a few minutes. "I got out and the guy next to me stepped on an IED. Caught some of the blast, messed up my leg." Clair's brows furrowed as she listened to him. For some reason, Charles kept rambling. "If that wasn't bad enough, we were being shot at too." Unconsciously, he winced as his hand went to his left shoulder at the memories. "Took a bullet, along with a few of my unit." He glanced up at her. "Oh, I, ah, I left on medical discharge after I healed up. My leg got pretty messed up, something about permanent nerve damage. But it doesn't bother me too much."

Clair gave him an encouraging smile, and his heart practically stopped. "I want to be an actress." She paused. "My brother tells me I can do it, but I don't believe him. I mean, I live in the middle of Missouri. I can't possibly be successful."

"My friend, Carmine, he's an actor, you know. Maybe I could ask him if he could get you some auditions or something?" he asked.

"Really? Stage or screen?" she inquired. She tipped the coffee back to finish it.

"Stage. He does Shakespeare in the Park every year. And he does a few other local productions during the rest of the year. He went to the University here and got a theater arts degree while I was over in the sandbox getting shot at. He tried to go into the military too, but they wouldn't let him." Charles remembered how upset Carmine had gotten over the fact they refused to let him enlist. "So, he stayed here, and did what he's good at. I mean, he's really good, too. His mentor offered to put in a word in some big studios for him if he wanted. But he stayed here in St. Louis. Kinda a shame, I think he could make it big if he tried. He's really talented," he mused as he finished his own coffee. Now, without a drink, he felt even more awkward sitting here with her.

When Clair didn't move to get up or leave, Charles realized that things were going better than he had hoped. He had been sure that she would have been in a rush to get out of here. Instead, she sat there, passing her empty cup back and forth between her hands.

"Why's he staying here, anyway? If he could make it in the big screen business?"

Charles sighed. "His mom. She's all he's got, you know? She raised him alone, and it wasn't easy for them. His mom's white, and he never knew his dad. But his dad was black. He doesn't fit anywhere, he says. So, he stays here to take care of his mom. She's got some medical problems. I think he said she's got some disease that limits her movement, something neuropathy or something like that. She's also got diabetes which is related to it. She's really nice, though. I practically lived in their kitchen growing up. So much food... So much. It isn't any wonder I had to work so hard to get in shape once I got in the military." He smiled at the memories. "Ms. Deangelo is some kind of cook..."

"Deangelo?" Clair sounded surprised. "That's your friend? Carmine Deangelo?"

"Yeah, you seen him in something?" He gave her a proud smile. He was always so proud of Carmine when someone remembered him.

"Oh, yes, I saw him in Hamlet at Shakespeare in the Park this summer. He was amazing as Laertes. Before that he played Mercutio in a small stage production of Romeo and Juliet I saw at the University." Clair blushed a little. "I'm sorry, I'm a sucker for Shakespeare, if I can make it to any production, I'll go, even high school plays."

"That's cool, I go to all Carmine's shows, at least on opening night. He gets me seats up front with his mom. He's going to be doing Much Ado later this year, October I think. I forget where though."

There was a short silence. "I wonder if you might want to have dinner." Clair locked eyes on him. "I'm free this weekend."

Charles felt his face redden and he nodded, a goofy grin spreading across his face. "Oh, yeah, sure."

## His Request

*A Few Months Later*

After a few months of dating, including attending many movies and plays, Charles decided to find out if she would be willing to join him in the Lifestyle. He was still certain of his decision not to participate in the Lifestyle with others he was not romantically involved with. It had not been easy. These days, he would only go with Carmine or Sasha, but he would only ever watch. If Clair decided not to join him, he would learn to live without the Lifestyle. Either way, her mere presence was enough to calm him most days. There were times when he needed something more fulfilling, and he wanted her to be the one to give it to him. He wanted her to claim every single part of him, from his mind to his body. More than that, he was never more surein his life that he was in love. If he could get her to agree, it would be the thing to make him whole.

After a movie date one evening, they were having dinner at a restaurant and discussing the movie. With Carmine's help, Charles had become a lot more knowledgeable about film and drama. He'd gone from not knowing the basics of how movies were made to understanding stage directions and different types of lighting. There was a pause in their conversation, and Charles started staring at his hands in hesitation. He was gathering his thoughts and every ounce of courage he had for what he was about to say.

"Charles, is there something wrong?"

He looked back up at her and took a deep breath before speaking. "I think I love you, Clair," he began. She looked at him in surprise and started to speak. "Wait, hear me out, okay? And if you aren't okay with it, I won't fault you. I just can't hold off any more, and I have to know. If you say no to what I'm asking, fine, I'll live. I'll figure it out and never ask again, but regardless you need to know about it."

Clair nodded, tucking her hands under her chin. Around them, the restaurant buzzed and no one paid any attention to the couple in the corner booth. The waiter had brought them a refill on their drinks and their shared dessert. Charles had split the piece of chocolate cake as they sat adjacent to each other in the booth. He picked up the fork and tapped it at his lip for a second before he spoke.

"So, that first date we went on when I couldn't shut up, I told you about how I got medically discharged. I told you about the bomb, about the IED, and getting shot. I told you I got into alcohol and Carmine and Sasha, my two best friends, helped me get out of it," he blurted out all at once, then paused and took a deep breath. What was she going to think? "Well, I didn't get out of it the way a lot of people do. Carmine, he took me to this club. Sasha, I didn't tell you he was my superior in the army when I got injured. He went there too, and between the two of them, they showed me a way I could deal with my PTSD." He put the fork into his mouth and bit down on the tines before he moved it to rest against his bottom lip again. "See, the club, it's a BDSM club. I'm not like them; they're both Dominant. I'm submissive."

Clair tilted her head to the side thoughtfully. "You mean like bondage stuff."

He nodded. "Yeah, I dated a couple ladies from the club, and I learned some stuff. I found out that being tied up, as well as the pain from being hit or something, helps me focus and get through my anxiety and panic attacks. But I can't just do what Carmine does. He can go down and play with people he's not dating or anything. I need more. I need to be with someone I love and care about, not just some random woman. It's not about sex, but I can't say I mind sex with a beautiful woman." He put the fork down when he realized he was playing with it. Clair nodded at him to encourage him to continue. "So, I think I'm in love with you, Clair Jaeger, and as hard as it was to ask you out that first time this is even harder..."

"Charles, you didn't ask me out to start with. I believe I was the one who asked you out when you stumbled over the attempt." She smirked and leaned over to put a hand against his cheek.

He blushed and nodded. "Yeah."

"You want me to do this with you. Learn how to do this Domination thing," she stated, leaning back and sipping her tea slowly.

Charles gave another nod. "If...if you want. It would help me. It helps me deal with the flashbacks and the nightmares. I think it would also help you build confidence in a lot of ways. You don't think you can succeed but maybe this can help you with that." His blush deepened and he dropped his head in his hands. "I'm sorry, here I am asking you for this and we haven't even slept together yet, or even talked about it," he whispered.

There was a long pause in which Clair appeared to be thinking. "My brother is going to kill me," she muttered. She shook her head with a sigh. "I think I love you, too, Charles, so help me, I've never fallen for someone so fast. You're sweet, attentive, and you want to make me happy. You've never put a hand on me that I didn't want, and you've always been kind to others around you. I can tell a lot by how a person treats their servers." When the waiter came back, she smiled and thanked him as he picked up their dinner plates and left the check. "You are always good to those that provide you services. You are a good man, Charles Ruebern. If it is something to make you happy, I am willing to try."

Charles smiled and opened his mouth to reply but stopped when she held up a finger. "I'll make no promises. I'm not sure I can do what you want of me, but we'll see how things work out."

His Bliss

*Present*

Thwack.

"Number," barked the hard voice.

"Ten, Mistress. Ten!" Charles yelped, shifting uncomfortably. His leg was starting to seize in its bindings. "Red," he gasped out, having reached his limit. "Leg."

Immediately, he felt Her arm wrap around him to lift him up enough to let him adjust his legs out from under him. She reached down and unsnapped the clip that connected his thigh cuffs to each other. Next, She unclipped the wrist cuffs from the back of his collar and let him put an arm around Her shoulders. She guided him to the nearby couch. She gently lowered him onto it before She sat down beside him and pulled him against Her. She began running Her fingers over the marks on his thighs. He leaned into Her grip and sighed deeply. "Mistress," he muttered as She stroked a hand over his head.

"I'm here, I'm here," She whispered. "You did wonderfully, such a good slave. You make Me so proud to own you, My love. So very proud."

His brown eyes rolled upward to meet Her blue ones. "Thank you, Mistress, thank you."

She pulled his body close to Her and in that moment, She was the only thing that existed. Her scent, Her taste, Her heartbeat... She was his everything.

# Resources

# Hotlines and Helplines

Here you will find a listing of resources compiled by the author on the following pages. At the time of this publication, resources are considered reliable and available. Please note this may change at any time, and the authors are not liable for the content of the following groups/resources. These resources relate to events in several of my books. They may be added to or altered at any time. Local resources may be available in your area. These are only a few of the possible resources for the following needs.

## Autism and Autism Self-Advocacy

## Autism Self-Advocacy Network

- info@autisticadvocacy.org

- http://autisticadvocacy.org/

## Autism Women's Network

- https://autismwomensnetwork.org/

## Identity First Autistic

- identityfirstautistic@gmail.com

- https://www.identityfirstautistic.org

## Mental Health and Mental Health Resources

## National Alliance on Mental Health

- 1-800-950-6264

- http://www.nami.org/

## Depression and Bipolar Support Alliance

- 1-800-826-3632

- http://www.dbsalliance.org/

## National Mental Health Association

- 800-969-6642

## Trauma/PTSD/Anxiety

## Anxiety Disorders of America

- 301-231-8368

## National Center for PTSD

- 802-296-5232

- https://www.ncptsd.org

## National Victim Center Infolink

- 800-FYI-CALL

## Eating Disorder Resources

## National Eating Disorders Association

- 800-931-2237 (M-F, 11:30 am-7:30 pm EST)

- http://www.nationaleatingdisorders.org/

## ANAD: National Association of Anorexia Nervosa and Associated Disorders

- 630-577-1330 (M-F,12 pm-8 pm EST)

- http://www.anad.org/

## Substance Use Disorder/Addiction Assistance

## Substance Abuse and Mental Health Services Administration

- 1-877-SAMHSA-7

- https://www.samhsa.gov/

## AL Anon Family Groups

- 800-344-2666

- 800-356-9996

- https://alanon.org/

## American Council for Drug Education

- 800-488-DRUG

- https://www.acde.org

## American Council on Alcoholism

- 800-527-5344

- https://assistedrecovery.com

## Harm Reduction Coalition

- 212-213-6376

- https://harmreduction.org

## National Institute on Drug Abuse (NIDA)

- https://www.nid.nih.gov

## Anonymous Groups

## Alcoholics Anonymous

- 212-870-3400

- https://www.aa.org

## Cocaine Anonymous

- 310-559-5833

- https://www.ca.org

## Co-Dependence Anonymous

- 602-277-7991

- https://www.coda.org

## Families Anonymous

- 800-736-9805

- https://www.familiesanonymous.org

## Gamblers Anonymous

- 213-386-8789

- https://gamblersanonymous.org

## Narcotics Anonymous

- 818-733-9999

- https://na.org

## Sexaholics Anonymous

- 866-424-8777

- https://sa.org

## Transgender Assistance and Equality

## Transgender Youth Equality Foundation

- 207-478-4087

- http://www.transyouthequality.org/

## Trans Student Educational Resources

- TSER@transstudent.org

- http://www.transstudent.org/

## Bullying Prevention Assistance

### Stopbullying.gov

- https://www.stopbullying.gov/

### PACERS National Bullying Prevention Center

- 1-800-537-2237

- http://www.pacer.org/bullying/

## Suicide Prevention Hotlines and Help

### National Suicide Prevention Hotline

- 1-800-273-8255

- https://suicidepreventionlifeline.org/

### Crisis Text Line

- Text "Start" 741-741

- http://www.crisistextline.org/

## Trans Lifeline

- US: 1-877-565-8860

- Canada: 1-877-330-6366

- https://www.translifeline.org/

## Suicide Prevention Resources

- http://www.sprc.org/

## The American Association of Suicidology

- http://www.suicidology.org/

## American Foundation of Suicide Prevention

- https://www.afsp.org/

## GLBT National Youth Talk

- 1-800-246-7743 (M-F, 4pm-12 am EST/Sat, 12 pm-5 pm EST)

## The Trevor Project

- 1-866-488-7386 (24/7)

- Text "Trevor" 1-202-304-1200 (F 4 pm - 8 pm EST)

- http://www.thetrevorproject.org/

## Warm Ear Line

- 1-866-WARM EAR (927-6327)

- http://warmline.org/

## Self-Injury Assistance

## S.A.F.E. Alternatives

- 1-800-DONTCUT

- http://www.selfinjury.com/

## Human-Created Disaster Helpline

## Disaster Distress Helpline

- 1-800-985-5990

- Text "TalkWithUs" 66746

## Sexual Violence and Abuse Resources

## National Sexual Violence Resource Center

- 1-877-739-3895

- http://www.nsvrc.org/

## RAINN- Rape, Abuse, and Incest National Network

- 1-800-656-4673 (National Sexual Assault Hotline)

- https://www.rainn.org/

## Domestic and Intimate Partner Violence Resources

## The National Coalition Against Domestic Violence

- 303-839-1852

- http://www.ncadv.org/

## The National Domestic Violence Hotline

- 1-800-799-SAFE

- http://www.thehotline.org/

## The National Resource Center on Domestic Violence

- 1-800-537-2238

- http://www.nrcdv.org/

## Human Trafficking Resources

## National Human Trafficking Resource Center

- 1-888-373-7888

- Text BeFree (233733)

## Runaway and Child Abuse Resources

## National Runaway Safeline

- 1-800-RUNAWAY (786-2929) (24/7)

- http://www.1800runaway.org/

## USA National Child Abuse Hotline

- 1-800-422-4453 (24/7)

## National Safe Place

- Text SAFE and your current location to the number 69866 (24/7)

- http://nationalsafeplace.org/

# About the Author
# Beverly L. Anderson

**She/Her or They/Them**

Beverly L. Anderson started writing at eleven, and when they did, it was apparent they would stick to something other than the every day. Her first story, written in spiral notebooks, was about a kidnapping. There were endless story ideas featuring fantastic places, monstrous creatures, and forbidden love in her mind even then. There's no surprise that these days, they favor the dark corners of the psyche over the happy and fluffy parts. Enamored with the mind, she studied extensively in psychology and related fields. She spends most of her days dreaming about stories and deciding how to make the unruly characters do as they tell them. As everyone knows, sometimes the characters take off and do what they want, no matter what the author has planned.

Beverly's other hobbies include gaming of all types, including a great love of tabletop, transgender and autism advocacy, and writing fanfiction when she can. Their interest in the BDSM community began as a simple curiosity but has led her to the road to finding a place for herself there as a Domme. She has gone on the journey of self-discovery in the last few years, finally pinning down their identity after nearly thirty years of searching. Coming out as bigender, asexual, panromantic, and polyamorous was one of the hardest things they've ever done, but it gave them the confidence to become themselves even more. An autistic person and an eclectic pagan, Beverly finds themself at odds with a lot of what society calls "normal." They don't mind, though, because they find that they are uniquely queer in every aspect of her life, and she's just fine with that.

Beverly started their writing journey seriously in 2013 when she found their way to fanfiction. She spent several years writing over three million words in various fandoms. In the last few years, they have been drawn to making those stories into original pieces and publishing them for a wider audience. Finding her publishing home helped make that dream a reality, one that they try to help others find.

Visit online: https://www.phoenixreal.net/

phoenixreal.net
Queer Love

# ALSO BY BEVERLY L. ANDERSON

## Crimson Hunt - Behind the Red Part One

Kerry Graham surprises his father by coming out as gay and cross-dresser and possibly non-binary. Then again, when he starts performing in drag at a local Cabaret named The Red, where his cousin works as a tailor. He finds himself free and able to be himself in a world that has always treated him as an outcast. He's among people that understand him, and he can finally relax. At least, that's what he believes. Then, a dress arrives, seemingly an apology for a bit of bigotry from a shop clerk. No one thinks a dress can cause any harm, so he wears it under the stage lights. Things go awry, though, and Kerry wonders what could possibly be happening. A bounty hunter named Martin swoops in, convinced that he can be of aid in the situation. Along with Martin, there's an intrepid FBI agent named Zak on the trail of a pair of sadistic serial killers who target and manipulate young, attractive, feminine men like Kerry.

Kerry doesn't believe it at first. Can he be targeted by these people? Then, things start happening, and his phone and email is full of messages with horrible images of what these people plan to do to him. He's frightened but staunch in living his life. He is adamant that he won't let them win, no matter what they do to him. Still, as the manipulation and gaslighting continue from afar, he starts to doubt everything he's ever known. He begins to lose purchase on reality but finds that Martin and Zak ground him. He refuses to give in to their sadistic games, but in the end, he begins to wonder if his willpower is enough to keep these people away from him.

## Stolen Innocence - Doctor's Training Part One

When desperate criminals find an easy target in the autistic neurosurgeon Kieran Sung, the young doctor is soon at the mercy of a local Irish mob boss with perverse desires. Despite suffering at his hands, rescue finds him with relative quickness. Pulled unwillingly into circumstances that bring his world crashing down around him and destroying the carefully laid routines and structure he desires; Kieran must find a new way to live. He discovers comfort in ways he never imagined, within sensations of pressure and binding. Taking the hand of a childhood friend who desires nothing else but to help him, Kieran realizes his heart aches for more in his life. Circumstances bind him to a tattoo artist named Varick Jaeger, an actor named Carmine DeAngelo, and a bartender named Devan Sullivan. With this unlikely trio, Kieran must learn how to handle the upheaval in a life he sees desperately needs change.

Stolen Innocence, part one of the Doctor's Training Trilogy, is a story of healing that examines D/s culture, the complexities of polyamory, and how people often deal with mental and physical trauma. Follow Kieran, Devan, Varick, Carmine, and the rest of their pack; they navigate a world that rarely accepts people who do not fit in with expectations.

## Escaping Fate, Embracing Destiny

CJ Kim is a normal college student. He is doing what most college students do, figuring himself out, sometimes the hard way. He has some strange dreams now and then, but he just thinks they are just dreams. They're certainly nothing to worry about when reality is pressing down so hard on him. Between the demands of school and family, he has enough on his mind.

He ends up with a huge crush on a senior that is on the baseball team. He doesn't even like baseball, but he goes to games just to see him. Of course, he'll never notice a gay and nerdy English major like CJ. Things are good, though. He even has a good relationship with his parents and his twin sisters.

He never expects his family's past to come back to haunt him. It rears its head in the worst way possible and CJ finds himself the prisoner of a vengeful man. Thrust into something that goes beyond what can be considered normal, CJ finds out that there's a fate out there trying to destroy him. He doesn't know how, but he has to reach for a destiny that he can just barely see.

## Dark and the Sword – Legacy of the Phoenix Book One

The world of Avern has moved on. It has been almost a thousand years since the day the entire pantheon disappeared. Since the Abandonment, the mortals have learned to live without gods and goddesses. The world became mundane, with little magic and even less hope. Tyrants have risen, and those able to wield what is left of magic are powerful. Forces surge in the darkness that threaten to topple the already fragile world. However, the plight of the world of Avern is not unknown, and those who watch from a distance have decided to intervene. The mortals are sleeping, however, unknowing that two great powers will soon be vying for control.

Then something happens that changes things. A young princess makes a bid for power by murdering her father. She then attempts to murder her sister, the crown princess of Lineria, Keiara. Despite a true strike aided by dark powers, Kciara doesn't die. Instead, the strike pierces the barrier between her human soul and the soul sleeping within her, the soul of the Dark Phoenix. More than a goddess, the Dark Phoenix is the legendary mother of the gods. She is a part of the Eternal Phoenix that brought life to their world eons ago, one of the primal forces of the cosmos.

## Chasing the Silver Dragon – Part One Disconnect, Book One of the Dragon Trinity Cycle

Silver Dragon has become a bane to the werewolf community in recent years. Designer heroin, one that actually affects were creatures where normal drugs are simply a passing fancy, has infiltrated the St. Louis werewolves. One of these, a young woman named Anna Maddox, wants her brother back somehow from the brink he's standing at. To do this, she reaches out to the ancient order, the Children of Asclepius. Duncan Powell hears her plea and pledges to help her rescue her brother from the streets of St Louis.

He goes to Detective Sebastian Pearce, a member of Unit Zero, the law enforcement agency that deals with supernatural creatures that pose a threat to the peace in the world. Sebastian implores him to leave things to Unit Zero, but Duncan is stubborn and goes down to the Red District to find the young Were. Sebastian and his partner follow and then begin the mission that will either save Kacey Maddox or doom all of them.

## Let Sparks Fly – Short Story Compilation

Romance can come from the most unexpected places. Sometimes, two people meet, and the sparks just fly between them. Then, sometimes, two people see each other every day, and don't realize the spark that exists between them.

In this volume, you will find stories of many kinds. You'll meet a pair of fellows just looking for a sub to share when they ask out two people, and a secret is revealed. A young man is pining for his very best (straight) friend when a strange entity shows him pleasures beyond imagining, along with some truth. Join a guy who secretly harbors a taboo wish he thinks will never come true. Watch the sparks as a pair of swimming rivals find themselves in a compromising position. A demon on a mountain demands a sacrifice and receives something he isn't expecting. And finally, a man finds his bliss in a woman who can completely own him.

Journey through these pages and enjoy short erotic stories of love found in some quite unusual ways.

## Whispered Shadows – A Poetry Anthology

The twisting paths of a poet's mind lead to intriguing places, there can be little doubt of this. These places contain whispers of the writer's soul. Some paths show desired sights; others uncover unforeseen knowledge and, at times, unwanted things. The shadows conceal unknown discoveries on well-lit paths through the poet's mind. Travelers, beware: uncertain destinations await along these paths. Tread carefully. Becoming lost in the pages of the poet's thoughts may be a very real danger to these travelers.

So, come along and visit this place of shadows. Here, there be dragons, monsters, truth, and more to enjoy. Fantasy, Reality, and Truths form one hundred and fifty poems by Beverly L. Anderson. The first path is one of fantasy with mythic beasts of yore and darkness that creeps into the very bone. Fairies may fly, and dragons may soar. The second path is one of reality and perhaps questions of what is and is not within that reality. Questions of existence and what the world shows us daily are spoken here. And the final path is one of truths. These truths may be surprisingly uncomfortable or may not be the truth expected. In any case, travel the paths at your own risk.

Open these pages and see if something draws you into the whispered shadows of the very soul.

## Reflections of the Shadow Dancer

In an abandoned dance studio, there's music and dancing unheard and unseen by anyone. The whispers in the shadows laud praises upon the figure who spins around the room, her body translucent and flickering in the night. Nothing is in motion, and yet everything moves around the room. Darkness and light intertwine and dance to cast the shadows of the world. The Shadow Dancer performs a dance that crosses the borders between the world and other surprising places within flickering shadows.

The Shadow Dancer knows the truth. Without the darkness, there can be no light. Without the light, there can be no darkness. Between them lies the shadow in which the Shadow Dancer twirls.

Enter the world of the Shadow Dancer and immerse yourself in 150 poems, living in the light, the dark, and the shadow.

current King of Hell. His mind is only clear when he is inside his own head and his world is spinning out of control. A terrible experiment that went wrong has left him on the verge of death, and it is up to the Codex of Hell and Addariel to save him.

Then, the strangest things happen among the demons. They devote themselves to his salvation, claiming him as their mate and, more than that, dedicating the hearts they didn't know they had to him. In his madness, he captures their very souls and changes the nature of the beasts around him. Even Addariel, once only interested in power, shifts his focus to taking care of the mentally fragile Bellamy. For the first time in Zion's history, the King of Hell cares more for something other than power and conquest.

Elysium, though, is not letting go of him easily. In a misguided attempt to help him, they make a move that could destroy the fragile peace between Zion and Elysium.

## Transcended by Earth – Chains of Blood Book Three

Rescuing Bellamy has become a priority for both Elysium and Zion. Adding to the mix are the Arcadians, who will stand to fight for Bellamy. Held by the angel Usiel in a location no one knows, Bellamy fights for his survival and the survival of his unborn child. Usiel wants to breed an army of angels capable of fighting demons without fearing their use of negative energy, and by doing that, he needs to rid Bellamy of the demon's child within him.

A human woman senses something off with a strange neighbor and investigates the situation. What she finds shocks her, and she knows what she must do. Taking Bellamy, unstable as he is, she flees, unsure what to do with what she thinks is a young girl pregnant with her a child her captor wishes to kill.

Meanwhile, in Arcadia, angels from Elysium and demons from Zion work together with a pirate radio station to try and find the missing Nephilim. The world is unsure, but they know they must find him before Usiel captures him again.

# Coming Soon – Chains of Blood

## From Beverly L. Anderson and J. Foster

**The Chains of Blood Trilogy**

**Confined by Heaven – Chains of Blood Book One**

The day started as any other day would. Bellamy Delacroix was shopping with his brother, and then he headed home to the inevitable discussion about his future with his mother. A woman who still cooks despite technology that doesn't require her to, his mother is an old-fashioned type in a future world.

Then, his world explodes quite literally, and he's swept up into a world beyond his imagination. A war between extraplanar creatures who call themselves angels and demons draws him in because of what he is. And what he is, no one has ever seen before—a Nephilim. He is the child of an angelic mother and a demonic father and is thus capable of channeling both the positive and negative energies of the planes. This makes him dangerous and a target for both the minions of heaven and hell.

An angel named Saniel takes him under her wing and helps him adjust as he is brought to the underground city of heaven, Elysium. He learns about what he is, who they are, and their enemies in Zion, the demons. A warning from an ally of his mother, though, rings in his head, and he wonders who he should really be trusting. Things begin to spiral in ways he doesn't understand, and the world is changing before his very eyes.

## Released by Hell – Chains of Blood Book Two

Driven insane by the very people he trusted, Bellamy is caught between worlds in a way like never before. He's in the hands of Addariel, the angel both at fault for his fall from grace and the